Noth[illegible] al to another man, [illegible] get Delaney marrying his Puritan cousin Abigail. And nothing, it seems, can save her from succumbing to the intruding Royalist's dark magnetism. Almost too late, she discovers his real, callous reason for marrying her – he has wagered that he will make her love him.

Can Abigail continue to live with Paget as a maiden wife, and tolerate the presence of the beautiful 'housekeeper' with whom he spends his time, when he has already won his wager?

The Passionate Puritan

Belinda Grey

MILLS & BOON LIMITED
London . Sydney . Toronto

First published in Great Britain 1978 by Mills & Boon Limited, 17-19 Foley Street, London W1A 1DR

ISBN 0 263 72718 1

Filmset in 11 on 12pt VIP Plantin

Made and printed in Great Britain by
C. Nicholls & Company Ltd
The Philips Park Press, Manchester

CHAPTER ONE

IT was nearly time for family prayers, but Abigail lingered by the window of her room, gazing out across the garden to the river that flowed past. As always the view enchanted her, for no other buildings obscured the magnificent sunsets that splashed themselves against the sky. A Jacob's ladder shimmered its golden rungs over the rippling river, and through the open casement a soft breeze gentled her cheek.

Although she was unaware of it she made a charming picture as she sat there, the deep mullioned window framing her slim figure and pale face, its delicate bones emphasised by the widow's peak in which her smooth brown hair grew. Under the peak her large brown eyes regarded the world with a lively curiosity that not all her father's lectures had been able to curb. She made a small face as she recalled his latest outburst.

Earlier that day she had slipped out of the parlour where she was polishing the silver and run out into the orchard, drawn by the bright sunshine and the desire to be out in all the loveliness of leaf and blossom and not tied to a dull, domestic task in the little panelled room. Under her feet the grass had been soft and springy and in sudden joy, merely at being alive, she had pulled up her skirts and begun to dance. Turning in wider and wider circles she had stopped at last, her arms flung about the trunk of an apple tree, her face lifted to the sunlight dappling the leaves, and heard her father's coldly disapproving voice.

"Abigail! What reason have you for this unseemly conduct?"

"I was – happy, father," she said breathlessly, twisting about to face him.

"Praised be the Lord for it then!" he returned. "But the Lord is not to be praised by wanton leaping and twirling. He is to be praised upon our knees with heads bowed in humility."

"Yes, father." She lowered her eyes, her lips still quivering with suppressed laughter.

"I am only thankful," her father said sternly, "that Thomas was not here to witness such levity. He would be inexpressibly shocked. In a child one might overlook it, but you are twenty years old and soon to be wed."

"Yes, father." There had been a faint weariness in her subdued reply.

"Have you leave to be out of doors?" he asked.

"No, father."

"Then return to your duties in the house. I will not mention this to your lady mother, for she has much on her mind just now. I fear that the return of Charles Stuart will affect us all."

It was Charles Stuart of whom she was thinking now as she gazed out across the tranquil garden. They would have to remember in future to call him King Charles the Second, for as such he would reign now that Parliament had recalled him from his eleven-year exile.

Abigail had only been nine years old when they had executed King Charles the First, but she could remember her father offering up thanks for the removal of the tyrant and the end of the wars that had set brother against brother, father against son. Now, in this month of June, sixteen hundred and sixty, everything was turned around again. The Protector Cromwell had died and, the army had, with Parliament's consent, invited Charles Stuart to return and sit upon his father's throne.

"For Charles the Tyrant is become Charles the Martyr," Thomas had said, "and men deny their deepest beliefs for the sake of advancement."

Thomas would never be false to his ideals, Abigail knew. He was four years older than she was, but had always seemed graver than other young men. With him she felt safe and cherished, her life flowing before her as uneventfully as the river that passed the garden and wound towards the great city of London.

The gong that summoned the Lane household to prayer twice a day sounded now, echoing hollowly through the small manor house. Lane House was a modest building, much smaller than the mansion where Uncle Henry Delaney lived.

Abigail had been to Delaney Court once and still remembered, with an inward shudder, the great pile of frowning stone, the long avenues of close-clipped yews, the portraits that followed her with their eyes. Her mother's brother she recalled as a tall, cadaverous man with a forked beard, who had stared at her from under beetling brows and demanded that she recite a psalm for him.

The gong reverberated again and she sprang up, smoothing down the few tendrils of hair that had strayed from beneath her white linen cap. Around her waist, over the full skirt of russet wool, was tied a neat white apron, and her laced bodice had cuffs and deep pointed collar of white lawn.

"A modest maid, modestly dressed," Thomas often

said, and his blue eyes were admiring as he kissed her cheek.

The turquoise betrothal ring on her left hand gave him the right to embrace her at meeting and parting. Sometimes, when he had gone, Abigail had a lonely, empty feeling as if something for which she had been waiting had passed her by, leaving her still untouched. She told herself that it would be different after they were married, and, glancing at the pretty blue stone, hurried through her parents' chamber and down the staircase to the hall out of which the parlour led.

Her father was already standing by the desk on which lay the open Bible, and he frowned towards the clock as she came in.

Her mother was kneeling by her high-backed chair and the servants were ranged against the wall, their hands folded.

Abigail folded her own hands, assumed an expression of polite attention, and went to her own place.

"Let us pray."

Josiah Lane's rich, deep voice rolled over his wife, Jessica, and his daughter. His eyes, resting on them, were troubled, but his tone held its usual calm certainty.

A Parliament man all his life, he had never doubted the rightness of his convictions. He had served bravely under General Ireton in the Civil War, emerging with a slight limp as the result of a sword thrust, and a pension from the government which enabled him to live in modest comfort with his wife and daughter. The return of the king would alter many circumstances and not, he feared, for the better.

"– in the name of Christ Jesus, our Lord, Amen."

He signalled with his hand that they might sit and,

closing the Bible, raised his head, sweeping them with his grave thoughtful glance.

"Mistress Lane and I received very sorrowful news earlier this day," he said. "Master Henry Delaney, my wife's brother, has died at his estate near Windsor. He had been sick some little time, but he died in the mercy of the Lord. His son, Paget Delaney, returned from France last month and sent word that he will visit us this evening. So we will have an extra place laid at table for supper, Temperance."

"Yes, Master Lane." The maid bobbed a curtsy.

"You may go to your duties now," Josiah said.

Abigail could scarcely contain herself as the servants filed out. That her father should admit under his own roof the wild cousin whose name was never mentioned both shocked and excited her. Paget Delaney had been only seventeen years old when he had run away to join the Cavalier army, and since that time all she had heard of him had been that he had fled to France with other supporters of the King and that Uncle Henry Delaney refused to acknowledge that he even had a son any longer.

"Is it really true, father? Is Paget Delaney coming here?"

"I am not in the habit of telling falsehoods," Josiah said. "Paget Delaney is visiting us this evening. And now that your curiosity is satisfied, perhaps you will have the good manners to express some sympathy with your lady mother on her bereavement."

"I own I cannot feel any deep sorrow," Mistress Jessica admitted. "Henry was several years my senior and we were never very close. Indeed, he had been practically a recluse for years."

"I remember going to Delaney Court once," Abigail

said. "It was a very grand house. There were trees cut into different shapes there."

"My brother was a very wealthy man," Jessica said, "Indeed I must confess that we had hopes—"

"We have no way of knowing yet whether your brother cut Paget out of his will," Josiah interrupted.

"And we are going to receive him here?"

"Out of politeness. He is, after all, your mother's nephew and your cousin." His voice was severe.

"Am I to change my dress?"

"You will wear your black gown tomorrow," he said. "Your cousin's servant rode here with the message only two hours ago, so Paget must take us as he finds us. I am prepared to meet him with moderate courtesy, but that must not be taken to mean that I condone his undutiful behaviour."

"I believe I can hear someone," Jessica said, patting her hair nervously. "Do you think we ought to go out to greet him?"

"I will go. You had better stay here," Josiah instructed.

"This news has come as a shock," Jessica confided as her husband left the room. "It is many years since I saw Henry, but he did write from time to time."

"And Paget?" Abigail queried.

"I met him once or twice when he was a boy," Jessica remembered. "I believe he was a sullen, difficult child, but I must confess that I did not expect him to turn traitor."

"Traitor?" Abigail looked at her, struck by a new idea. "Since the King came back we are the ones who are traitors, surely?"

The parlour door opened again and Josiah came in, his face drawn into lines of disapproval.

Abigail's eyes flew past him to the tall, broad-shouldered figure who had paused on the threshold, feathered hat in his hand. Long black hair framed a lean, dark face out of which light grey eyes raked her insolently from head to foot. Out of deference to his father, she supposed, his suit was of black, but there were frills of white lace at his throat and wrists, and as he bowed she glimpsed a diamond earring glinting among his dark locks.

"Paget, I wish to present you to my lady wife and my daughter, Abigail," Josiah said stiffly.

"Aunt Jessica!" The man stepped forward, kissing her hand. "I recall you when I was a child. And this is Abigail? You were only a babe when I saw you, and I declare you are vastly improved since that time!"

His carefree tone and broad smile annoyed her intensely, for she sensed a challenge in his attitude towards her. There was no denying that he was attractive, but she was determined not to be cozened by such disrespectful admiration.

"Master Delaney, we were sorry to hear of your father's death," she said, as coolly as she could though the blood had rushed to her face.

"Paget," he corrected, holding her hand a fraction longer than was necessary. "We are cousins, you and I. My father's death was not entirely unexpected – save by himself. He neglected to make a will cutting me out of my inheritance, so despite his vow never to acknowledge me again as his son, Delaney Court will revert to me."

Abigail, glancing at her parents, saw sick disappointment in their eyes. Paget saw it too, for she noticed his smile grow broader.

"We had best go in for supper," Jessica said at last,

swallowing hard. "The meal is only a simple one, but you gave little warning of your arrival."

"I am a creature of impulse," Paget said airily. "My man delivered the message, I take it?"

"And rode away again, though he was offered refreshment."

They had emerged into the raftered hall and Josiah motioned the guest to a seat at the long table.

"Robin prefers the roistering of the tavern to the gossip of the kitchen," Paget said.

"My own servants are not permitted to frequent alehouses," Josiah said coldly. "Shall we say grace?"

Bowing her head, Abigail could not resist a swift, upward glance to where her cousin sat opposite her. His own eyes were fixed upon her and there was a coldly considering gleam in them that made her suddenly uneasy.

"Will you have trout, sir, or mutton pie?" Temperance was asking as Josiah's last 'Amen' resounded about the table.

"Trout, my love," Paget said, and the maidservant let out a startled giggle.

"Go back to your seat, Temperance. We will serve ourselves," Josiah said.

"Trout from the river is an excellent start to a meal." Unabashed, Paget helped himself liberally. "His Majesty is very fond of it, served with a salad of fennel and parsley."

"You know Charles Stuart?" Abigail could not help asking the question.

"I have split a bottle of malmsey with him on one or two occasions," he returned. "Mind, none of us could afford the best wines while we lived as pensioners in the courts of France and Holland!"

"It was your own actions that sent you into exile," Josiah said severely.

"True, but you cannot blame me for having grumbled a trifle when the winter was so cold that we had to stay abed all day to save fuel," Paget said. "There is a limit to the pleasures that even I can find between the sheets."

Abigail's mouth dropped open in horror. Never had she expected to hear such coarse sentiments uttered at her father's table. She dared not look at him or her mother. Her cousin, apparently unaware of his lapse in taste, was eating the fish calmly, mentioning the fine bouquet of the wine, praising the gooseberry preserve with its buttercream topping.

"Do you intend to make your home at Delaney Court?" Jessica was asking as they rose from the table.

"With my wife, yes."

So he was married! With all her heart Abigail pitied his wife.

"You did not bring her with you?" Josiah asked.

"As to that, sir, I would appreciate a word with you," Paget said. "With my aunt and cousin. This concerns them too."

"Very well." With a slightly puzzled air Josiah indicated the inner door.

"I will be as brief as possible," Paget said when they were seated in the parlour. A small fire had been kindled to offset the evening chill and its flames danced merrily on the raised hearth. "I spoke of my living at Delaney Court with my wife. In fact I am not yet married, but that is a circumstance I propose to remedy."

"Oh?" Josiah stared at him.

"I said that my father neglected to make a will, and

that was true," Paget continued. "However, he did leave a draft of his intentions. It was never witnessed and so has no validity in law, but I believe the wishes of the dead should be respected."

"That displays a very proper sentiment," Josiah said with grudging approval.

"I was certain you would think so." The brilliant grey eyes danced. "You were granted a pension, I believe, because of a war injury you suffered?"

"By the Protectorate, yes."

"And I imagine that pension will cease now that the regicides have been overthrown. I have also heard that known supporters of the illegal régime maybe fined quite heavily for their part in the conduct of the war."

"That's true." Josiah nodded reluctantly.

"My late father apparently intended to double your pension and pay your fine as well as his own," Paget said, "but, as I said, he left no will."

"We did have hopes," Jessica said tremulously.

"And I feel a certain responsibility in the matter," Paget smiled. "After all, if I had been killed in the war, you, aunt, as my father's next-of-kin, would have inherited Delaney Court itself. So I am willing to implement my father's wishes, to double your pension and pay any necessary fine, and take cousin Abigail to wife, without dowry."

There was an instant's pause. Then Abigail sprang up, her cheeks flaming.

"I am already betrothed!" she cried. "Even if I were not, you are the last person I would take as a husband."

"Daughter, be still!" Josiah too had risen. "Paget, I regret it but my daughter is betrothed. Surely you noticed her ring?"

"A ring can be removed," Paget observed.

"Thomas Wellborn is a fine young man," Abigail choked, "and I will not be forsworn."

"Who is this Thomas?" Paget enquired.

"A lawyer, promised to Abigail these four years."

"I always heard the law moved slowly," Paget said. "Is he blind, this Thomas, that he cannot see the bloom on a wench?"

"We agreed to wait until he had saved some money," Abigail said stormily.

"Well, you and I would have no need to wait," he said calmly, "for I am already very rich. My late father seems to have trebled his fortune over the past years. I have what might be termed an embarrassment of gold."

"But must look elsewhere for a wife," she retorted.

"Abigail, you must not push yourself forward into the conversation," her father reproved. "It is as she tells you, sir. She is pledged to Thomas Wellborn."

"A pledge can be broken."

"Not by me!" Abigail broke in furiously.

"Then we must persuade the gentleman," Paget murmured.

"Thomas would never agree!"

"Thomas is a lawyer, is he not? I never knew a lawyer yet whose palm could not be greased. Oh, we will strike a bargain, I've no doubt."

"If Thomas were dead," she ground out, "I still would not marry you."

"Then your parents must look elsewhere for pensions and the wherewithal to pay fines," Paget said. "I wish you would detail your objections to me."

"I could not love you," she said, "I could never love you!"

"Since when did people of quality wed for love?" He

raised thin black brows. "Love is for peasants – and poets."

"The girl is upset," Josiah said. His melancholy face displayed a growing alarm, and his fingers clenched and unclenched as if he felt the pension slipping out of them.

"Father! Paget Delaney is a King's man! A Cavalier! You wouldn't consider his proposal."

"Your father is thinking of the old proverb, 'Needs must when the devil drives'," Paget commented.

"If you are so rich, why cannot you be generous and give us what your father intended us to have?" she demanded.

"Because I am not generous," he said, and again the gleam in his eyes chilled her. "I spent eleven years in a miserable exile, my dear, where I took to heart one valuable precept. Never give without taking something in return! It is an excellent maxim."

"A godless one," she said.

"Ah, theology I leave to you Puritans," he assured her. "You all seem to have a back door into Heaven. You may rest assured that I will not interfere with your mode of worship. You may do the praying for both of us."

"But not as your wife. I'll never be that!"

"Uncle Josiah, you should have instilled obedience into your daughter," Paget said. "Isn't it written somewhere in that book my father used to quote at me that women should be meek and silent, obeying their masters?"

"You must be still," Abigail's mother pleaded. "This matter is for your father and me to settle."

"But there is nothing to settle," she persisted. "I am pledged to Thomas Wellborn. You cannot turn my whole life upside down for the sake of a pension."

"Doubled!" said Paget softly. He had not risen but lounged in his chair, long legs stretched before him, the firelight glinting on his buckled shoes.

"Treble it, and I'll still not have you!"

"That's a pity," he drawled, "for I have quite made up my mind to have *you*. I confess I'd prefer a willing bride, but an unwilling one might be amusing to tame. I'll be a good husband, you've no need to fear that I'd neglect or ill-treat you. And on each anniversary of our marriage I'll add an extra twenty sovereigns to your father's pension."

For a moment she was too angry to speak. Then she flung back her head, biting off her words as if they were thread. "Your exile has addled your wits, sir, or perhaps they are still savage in foreign courts! My parents would never sell me into a marriage as if I were a cow or a horse. And now I beg to be excused."

She wrenched open the door and went into the hall. The table had been cleared and she could hear the murmur of conversation from the kitchen as Temperance and Mercy washed the dishes.

There was a quick step behind her as she gained the stairs, and she turned and saw him standing, tall in the shadows, his teeth a white flash in the darkness of his face.

"I will have you, Cousin Abigail," he said softly. "Best make up your mind to it."

She twisted away from his detaining hand and ran up to the gallery. Her own fingers groped for the latch on the bedroom door and her breath came sobbingly, but above her hammering heart she could hear him chuckling in the hall.

Not until she was in her own chamber, with the bolt

drawn, did her panic subside. What was happening must be some monstrous dream, a ride upon the nightmare such as she had taken in childhood. It was simply not possible that a smiling, insolent relative, whose name had not been mentioned for years save in tone of hushed disapproval, could really be bribing her parents into agreeing to a marriage!

"I am pledged to Thomas Wellborn," she muttered defiantly, but his blue eyes and fair hair would not form clearly in her mind, and in her ears echoed that deep, amused laughter.

CHAPTER TWO

"YOU must try to understand my position," Josiah said. He spoke quickly, avoiding his daughter's eyes. "Now that Charles Stuart is back times will not be easy for those who supported the Parliament. I will lose my pension and the fines may be heavy. They say the King is short of money and will raise every coin he can."

"But to marry me to a man I despise!" Abigail choked.

"You have met him only once," her father said. "You cannot judge a man so speedily."

"For years his name has hardly been mentioned," she said, "and now he is not to be judged! If he had come back penniless – if Uncle Henry Delaney had made a will that disinherited him – you would not now be forcing me into wedlock."

"I force you to nothing," he interrupted. "I merely remind you of your duty."

"Is it my duty to wed a man whose behaviour is coarse and whose speech offends me? You heard the manner in which he talked, the way in which he mocks good people, even the faith in which we find our strength! You cannot mean me to be joined to such a man."

"I mean you to be realistic," Josiah said. "If justice were done then we would be moving to Delaney Court.

But Paget has inherited it and we are in a fair way to be beggared unless you decide to be sensible."

"You know that Thomas and I would help you in every way we could."

"Thomas is only now in a position when he can begin to support a wife, and he may never have enough to be able to live in luxury."

"We could work the land here," she said desperately.

"We grow enough to supply most of our household needs," he said with heavy patience, "but that's all. Everything else has to be squeezed out of my pension. When that ceases we would be in dire straits."

"We could let the servants go. Mercy and Temperance and Jem could find work elsewhere."

"And your lady mother could scrub the floors and scrape vegetables, while I dug the garden and groomed the horses, I suppose?" His voice was bitterly sarcastic.

"I don't want to compromise my ideals," she said in a low voice.

"And when you are on your pedestal will it content you to look down and see your parents reduced to penury? Will the Lord praise you as a dutiful child when you have set yourself up against our will and desire?"

"I do not love him," she said, her lower lip trembling.

"Affection grows after marriage," he returned. "Such obstinacy in a female astounds me, Abigail! I really begin to think that I made some terrible mistake in your rearing. We have given you too much freedom, I fear. We have taken pleasure in your intelligence and encouraged you to express your opinions. Why, I cannot think of another father who would allow his daughter to sit arguing with him in such a manner!"

He was working himself up into a cold rage, the veins at his temple swelling, his voice rising. Yet she guessed that his rage stemmed as much from fear as from anger at her obduracy. He had never been a wealthy man, but he was secure in his household. Now he was faced with possible ruin and he had no resources within himself to meet it.

"You had better go into the garden," he said thickly. "Look up to the heavens and beg your Creator to grant you a dutiful heart. I will speak to you again later."

Abigail withdrew silently. Her mother was usually lying down at this hour, and the garden was deserted. She crossed the stable yard and went into the narrow strip of orchard that ran down to the river bank. It was ironic to remember how gaily she had pirouetted here so short a time before. Now her feet were leaden and her eyes stung with unwashed tears.

Thomas Wellborn was riding along the river bank. She glimpsed his soberly clad figure between the trees and hurried to meet him, her heart lifting.

"Abigail." He dismounted, brushing her cheek with his lips, but one glance at his set, white face told her that he knew.

"Have you seen father?" she asked.

"I met your cousin," Thomas said. "I understand he was here last night."

She nodded, her anxious eyes on his face.

"Your father gave him my address and he called upon me this morning," Thomas said. "He tells me that he is determined to wed you."

"But I'll not have him!" she cried. "I told him, and I have told my parents, that I will never agree to marry him. They may drag me to the church door but I'll not speak the vows! I don't care what threats he chooses to make!"

"He has it in his power to ruin me," Thomas said flatly.

"To ruin –? But how?" Appalled, she stared at him, her hand dropping from his arm. "You never fought in the war! Nobody can fine *you* or take away *your* pension."

"He can take away my hope of practising law," Thomas said sombrely.

"But how?"

"By being a wealthy man and having the ear of the King. He has only to drop a few words into that royal ear and my licence to practice could be removed."

"He actually threatened that?"

"And it was no idle threat," Thomas said. "You know I have neither money nor influence as yet, but Paget Delaney has both, and will use them unscrupulously to gain his desires."

"Then we must be secretly wed," she said rapidly. "We don't have to stay in this country. We could sail to the New World. There are Puritans there and they need lawyers."

"And your parents? You know they would hate to leave England, and we could not, in conscience, leave them behind so that Master Delaney could wreak his vengeance on them."

"Then what are we to do?" she asked. "I am like a mouse in a maze with no way of escape."

"It touches me too," he said.

"Touches? No more than touches! Thomas, we have been betrothed these four years, pledged to love each other to the end of our days!" she cried. "Our lives are to be torn apart, and you say that it touches you!"

"Strikes deeper than I can express," he said slowly. "But I can see no hope for us, unless you submit."

It didn't seem possible that he could be speaking in such a fashion. The last secure thing in her fragile world tilted and slid away.

"My dear, we have to be brave," he was saying. She could hear each separate word quite clearly but they jumbled in her mind. "I cannot make a living at my profession if your cousin decides to prevent it, and he has made it clear that he will prevent it if I marry you, just as he will stand by and see your parents ruined without lifting a finger to help them. There is nothing to be done."

"Thomas! Thomas, don't talk like that, please?"

Words broke from her, but his blue eyes were remote, his face stiff with painful duty.

"I am going to see your father," he said, "I am going to tell him that I release you from our betrothal. It is the only honourable thing to do, for we cannot snatch our happiness at the expense of others."

"My ring." She began to draw it off in a distracted fashion, but he put his hand over hers, preventing it.

"Keep it or throw it away. I could not endure to take it back after what we have meant to each other."

He spoke as if everything was finished, as if four years could end as easily as one closed a book. She stood, her eyes wide with shocked disbelief, and watched him walk away from her, his fair head bowed, his shoulders hunched in misery.

It had never occurred to her for one moment that Thomas would give her up so easily, that he would yield to the pressures put upon him. Yet nobody could blame him, she thought fiercely. Paget Delaney was obviously a hard and unscrupulous man who allowed neither kindness nor conscience to stand in his way.

If she went back to the house now she would not be able to bear it. Her father would accept Thomas's going with ill-concealed relief and she would be left with no support in her lonely defiance.

Slowly, fighting back her tears, Abigail threaded her way through the trees to where the grass sloped down to the sun-glinted river. It was such a beautiful season with spring dancing, leaf-clad and blossom-crowned, into summer. She had hoped for so much and now it was spoiled. Her whole life was spoiled and the river still flowed uncaringly.

She stepped to its edge and looked down at the breeze rippled wavelets. There were long weeds twisting and turning below the surface and a fish quivered, silver-finned, out of the tangled stems. It would be so easy to slip down into that deep coolness and surrender completely to the despair that threatened to engulf her.

She took a step back, tugging at the ring on her finger, sobbing as she flung the golden circle with its blue stone into the water. It skimmed and then sank, and in a moment even the ripples had gone. A pale mark round her finger was like the ghost of the joy she had expected to know.

"Don't spoil your face with tears," a voice said behind her. "I'll give you a handsomer ring than that."

She turned, rubbing furiously at her wet cheeks, dismayed to find Paget Delaney standing in the shadow of one of the apple trees. He must have approached so quietly that she had not heard even his step upon the path.

"I want no ring from you," she muttered.

"But I intend to give you two rings," he said, coming forward. "Bracelets and earrings too. You ought to wear rubies and emeralds and amber to bring out the light in your eyes. Here, girl!"

For a moment she bristled, thinking that he was calling her, but he had whistled to Thomas's mare. The horse raised its head from the grass and trotted towards him, nuzzling his velvet coat as if it recognised a friend.

"Wellborn's mount?" Paget rubbed its nose gently. "Does he know no better than to leave a good animal untethered?"

"He had other things on his mind," she said icily.

"I caught a glimpse of the young man cutting across the orchard as I came down the garden," Paget said. "No, girl, I've no apple about me or sugar. Be off to your master and bear him safe to his lodging." He flicked the rein and patted the mare on its side as it moved away.

There had been gentleness in his voice when he talked to the horse, but his tone sharpened into mockery as he looked at Abigail.

"Very few women can cry prettily," he observed. "However I'll overlook your pink nose, for it's understandable you'll be a mite discomposed after such a sad parting. I assume it was a sad parting? When I spoke to Master Wellborn this morning he seemed quite resigned to the ending of your betrothal."

"You threatened to ruin him, to have his licence revoked so that he could no longer practise Law. I call that despicable!" she flashed.

"Do you, my love? I call it expediency," he said calmly.

"It will not gain you anything as far as I am concerned," she said, "I honour integrity and gentle conduct. You have offended against everything I was reared to believe is true and right. My opinion of you could not be lower!"

She broke off, checked by his laughter. He stood, hands on his hips, dark head flung back, and laughed at her. Her despair turned to such anger that a red mist blurred her vision and she sprang at him, her nails raking his lean, dark face. Her wrists were caught in a bruising grip and he shook her so violently that her head jerked backwards and forwards on her neck. For a moment she was as mindless and helpless as a doll, and then his mouth fastened savagely upon hers. The red mist dissolved and every colour in the world spun crazily behind her closed lids.

"I care nothing for your opinion," he said, releasing her so abruptly that she staggered. "I have a fancy to wed you, Cousin Abigail. When I came here yesterday I meant to marry you, but it was a relief to find out that you were comely. A man doesn't care to bed a plain female."

"You'll wed me because I have no power to prevent it," she whispered, "but you'll never bed me, save by force."

"A challenge? My love, I never could resist a challenge," he said.

The brief passion that had flared up between them was as quickly spent. His tone was hard and mocking again, and the gleam in his eyes chilled her. She rubbed her aching wrists and scowled at him, her eyes burning with contempt, not only at his behaviour but at her own reaction.

"I want you to leave," she said tremblingly. "I tell you, Master Delaney, that you may marry me, but you'll not enjoy it. You'll get no satisfaction despite your threats. You never will get anything from me except hatred."

"Which is always better than indifference," he said coolly. "I imagine Master Wellborn will be reunited with his horse by now and on his way home, so I'll bid you good-day and go and tell your father that we have reached an agreement."

"What agreement?" she demanded.

"You have agreed to hate me and I have agreed to marry you," he smiled.

"You show great wisdom in avoiding Thomas," she gibed. "He might be tempted to knock you down!"

"I don't think so. He had ample opportunity to 'Knock me down', as you so elegantly phrase it, when I visited him this morning, but he showed no inclination to do so. Lawyers are not noted for their physical courage," he returned.

"You know nothing about Thomas," she said.

"I think I know sufficient," he said. "Certainly I know enough about him not to be anxious for a more intimate friendship. But you may keep your good opinion of him if you choose."

"I'll do that without your leave," she said, and flinched despite herself as he came close again, taller and broader than either her father or Thomas, his wide mouth curving into a half-smile, his eyes holding her frightened brown ones in a brilliant, soulless gaze. There were feelings deep within her that bewildered and angered her, confusing her thoughts as the trailing weeds confused the still water beneath the rippling waves.

"After we are married," he said gently, "you will learn many things, my love, and I tell you that one of them will be how to please me. And I tell you further that slavish obedience does not please me either in dogs or women. Senseless defiance does not please me either. You must try to strike a balance between the two."

For an instant he leaned so close that she feared he was going to kiss her again, but he merely tapped her cheek with a long brown forefinger and walked away, his short black cloak swinging jauntily from his wide shoulders.

Weakly Abigail sat down on the grass, her legs shaking with what she assured herself was relief. Paget Delaney was abominable, she told herself, and his conduct was inexcusable. How her father could consent, even under threat, to her marriage with him was something she would never understand.

In so short a time, she reflected dismally, had she been forced into silence.

She waited until she was certain that both Thomas and Paget Delaney would have left, and then she walked back slowly to the house. It glowed like a jewel in the late afternoon sunshine, its green lawn circling it, its windows twinkling under the eaves.

Abigail had been born in this house, had grown up here in the security of its walls. She could remember how, when she was very little, her mother had taught her to read her letters from a hornbook. They had sat together in the garden and when the lesson was done they had gone down to the river and watched the birds sweep low over the water. Her father must have been fighting with the Parliament forces, but she had no real memory of the war. In this tranquil backwater the conflict had not touched them.

She remembered too how, in those days, her mother had been plumper and had smiled more readily. The years after the war, when her father's presence had quelled all gaiety, had crushed Jessica's natural optimism. Yet she had never uttered one word of complaint, perhaps because she was not aware of the reason behind her sadness.

"Daughter, why do you waste time in staring at the house?" Josiah demanded, emerging from the hall.

"I was just thinking," she said slowly, "how you would both hate having to leave here."

"Leave? But there's no question of our leaving," he said testily, "Thomas informs me that he has released you from your pledge."

"Because Paget Delaney made threats, just as he made threats against you," she said tightly.

"That cannot be excused," he admitted. "I make no excuse for it."

"But you are still willing for this marriage to take place?" she challenged.

"I see no other way," he told her. "I hope that you have decided to be sensible about the matter. I have been very patient with you, Abigail, when many fathers would not even have troubled to discuss the matter. As my daughter you are bound in duty to obey me, and I have the right in law to wed you to whomever I choose."

"You chose Thomas Wellborn," she said sadly.

"Paget Delaney is not," he admitted, "the man I would have picked for you. He does not share our faith or our ideals."

"But he is rich," she said. "He is rich and he can make life very hard for you if he is refused. Ideals have nothing to do with it."

"Abigail." For the first time in her life she heard a shamed pleading in her father's voice, but she steeled herself against it and walked past him into the hall.

Her mother had risen from her afternoon nap and called to her from the parlour. Jessica's face was drawn with anxiety, but she spoke cheerfully.

"So it is all arranged, then? Thomas made no difficulties and Paget arrived just after him to tell us you had accepted his suit."

"Unwillingly," Abigail said.

"It is very difficult for you," Jessica admitted, "but it may all turn out well in the end. I believe that Paget is not entirely beyond redemption."

"I haven't the slightest interest in performing the task," the girl said stonily.

"But you have agreed to wed him? You won't change your mind and anger your father by a show of disobedience?"

"I'll marry him," Abigail said briefly.

"It is not that we don't consider your feelings," Jessica ventured. "You are our only child, after all, and we want your happiness."

"Yes, of course." Abigail spoke wearily, for her head was beginning to throb.

"You know you could never be happy if any action of yours were to lead to our being miserable."

"I really don't wish to talk about it any further," Abigail said.

"But there are certain arrangements to be made," Jessica said. "We have agreed that the ceremony is to be performed early next month, and—"

"But that's only a fortnight away!" Abigail exclaimed in dismay.

"Paget wishes to take up residence at Delaney Court as quickly as possible. He has been away from his home for eleven years, we must remember."

"Because he ran away in the first place."

"You must try to display a more Christian spirit of forgiveness," her mother said.

"Oh, I forgot! Paget Delaney has inherited his father's wealth," Abigail said. "We must indeed forgive the rich!"

"Is the thought of this marriage so abhorrent to you?" Jessica looked upset.

"I've said I will go through with it. Feelings don't enter into the matter."

Abigail spoke coldly, but her delicate skin had flushed. She could still feel Paget's hard, demanding mouth forcing her own lips to part in surrender, and faint blue marks at her wrists were evidence of the tight grip in which he had held her. She was too honest to pretend to herself that the incident had not excited into life something that must lie hidden in her nature, for she had never suspected its existence until now. Perhaps her father was right when he said that all women were wantons at heart. Of one thing she was resolved. Never again would she allow Paget Delaney to break down the icy wall of defence with which she intended to surround herself.

"He left a present for you," Jessica said.

"Who? Thomas?"

A keepsake, no matter how modest, would soothe her wounded feelings, for she could not help thinking that Thomas had given in too easily.

"No, my dear. Paget." Jessica indicated a flat box on the table. "He said it was a betrothal gift."

Abigail opened it slowly and could not resist a gasp of pleasure. Against black velvet an exquisite necklace of golden topazes glowed warmly, each stone set in gold links. The workmanship was delicate and so finely wrought that she guessed it must have been fashioned by a master craftsman.

"They're beautiful!" Jessica had risen from her chair and was gazing at them with frank delight.

"Baubles," Abigail corrected. "You know we are bidden to wear modest garments. It is one of the tenets of our faith."

"It is also written that a wife should obey her husband," Josiah said, coming into the room. "Paget will expect you to wear them on your wedding day."

"They will look magnificent with the cream silk," Jessica said.

"Not my wedding gown!"

Tears of protest flooded her eyes. She had worked the gown herself and it was laid in lavender ready for the day when she would marry Thomas. High-necked and long-sleeved with a dipped waistline and flowing skirt, it was the prettiest dress she had ever owned, and she often imagined Thomas's quiet smile of approval when he saw her wearing it. Now to have to wear it for her marriage to Paget Delaney was a dreadful thought, as if she were displaying all her hopes and dreams before his mocking gaze.

"There isn't any time to make a new gown," Jessica said, "even if we could afford it. I'm thankful you're well supplied with shifts and nightgowns."

"There are more important aspects of marriage than clothes," Josiah frowned. "I hope you will find time to instruct Abigail in the duties of a wife."

"Yes. Yes, of course." As always when her husband spoke to her, Jessica wilted a little. To Abigail she said fussily, "Now do put the necklace away safely, dear."

"I'll take it up now." Glad of the opportunity to

escape, Abigail lifted the box and went swiftly to her room.

Her wedding gown was in a chest under the window. She knelt, lifted the lid, and smoothed its creamy folds with her hand. It was a lovely dress, and every stitch had been put in it with thoughts of Thomas Wellborn. Sadly she added Paget's gift and closed down the lid.

Two weeks more and she would be Mistress Delaney, married to a man who would stop at nothing to get what he wanted. And marriage, as her father had reminded them, involved more than pretty gowns. It involved an intimate relationship to which the woman submitted for the purpose of begetting children.

Her heart beat faster and her mind shivered away from the pictures rising up in it. Thomas had always respected her innocence, but she feared that Paget respected nothing. Certainly he had no affection for her and no interest in her happiness, else he would not have forced her into this betrothal.

After the wedding she would be subject to him as she was now subject to her parents. Her lips thinned into a narrower line as she rose.

They might force her to marry Paget Delaney, but under no circumstances would she prove a docile bride.

CHAPTER THREE

ABIGAIL woke on her wedding day with a feeling of deep depression weighing down her spirits. Rather to her surprise she had slept deeply and dreamlessly, but her eyes opened upon the dress, hanging against the wall under its shield of net. The little cap of pleated white silk from which a modest veil depended had been put on the table near to the box containing the topazes.

On her right hand was the betrothal ring that Paget had sent her the previous day. He had not called upon them at all since their meeting down by the river and, while she had been heartily glad at his absence, part of her deeply resented the fact that he had not troubled to pay her any of the attentions a gentleman usually paid his betrothed. The ring was a square-cut emerald in a heavily-chased gold setting.

"One of my brother's rings," Jessica had commented. "Paget must have had it made smaller. It's very handsome."

Handsome but too ornate, Abigail decided. When the stone caught the light it gleamed cold and sinister. The simple turquoise, now lying at the bottom of the river, had suited her better.

At least it would be a very quiet ceremony. They were to be married in the local church where she had always attended Sunday services, and there would be no wedding breakfast as they were to ride at once on the three-day ride to Delaney Court. The Lanes were reserved people with few friends, and Abigail had been kept so close to home that she had never had companions of her own age.

"You are not still unhappy, are you?" Jessica enquired when she had brought in the ale and salt bacon and fresh-baked rolls on which Abigail, for once in her life, was to breakfast in her own room. "I do assure you that we would never force you to anything unless we had no other choice."

They could have chosen to be poor, Abigail thought cynically, but she contrived a small smile as she answered, "I am quite ready to wed Paget Delaney."

"And you must not be alarmed if he wishes to take certain liberties. Such actions are part of the marital state and must be endured if we are to fulfil our obligations," Jessica said.

Abigail murmured something and pushed a fugitive bit of bacon around her plate. The smell of the breakfast was slightly nauseating and there was a fluttering in the pit of her stomach.

"I'm sure he will be kind," her mother was saying. "Of course he is ten years older than you are, and a man of thirty is usually – experienced, but that need not be such a bad thing. He will probably be very considerate."

Abigail doubted it, but she made another indeterminate noise and gulped her ale. It was well watered and pleasantly sour, but it was an effort to swallow.

The ceremony was to take place at ten. By nine she was dressed, the creamy silk outlining her high breasts and tiny waist and falling to the tips of her bronze shoes. Her hair had been combed back from its widow's peak and coiled at the nape of her neck, and the silk cap with its veil framed her small face becomingly. Jessica took the necklace, clasped it about her daughter's neck and stood back, admiration in her face.

"You look – oh, my dear, you look lovely," she breathed. "I know vanity is a sin, but you have cause to be proud of your appearance today. Now, where is your cloak? The roads are dusty and we don't want your gown to be smeared."

Abigail could not prevent a small flicker of triumph. At least she looked desirable, and even that triviality was a comfort to her spirits. Pride would not allow her to appear crushed or woebegone. She was being forced into this marriage, but she would walk up the aisle with her head high.

They had only a short distance to walk to the church, and it was a fine day. Abigail, glancing at the ornate betrothal ring, thought rain would the better have matched her mood. Her horse was to be brought round to the church in readiness for the start of their journey, and her clothes had already been loaded on to a pack mule. They would not be returning to the house, and she looked about her bedroom with a lost, bewildered feeling, noting the remains of her breakfast on the tray, the tumbled blankets, the empty cupboards. Already the chamber had the slightly sordid aspect of an abandoned room.

"It's time we were leaving," Josiah said, tapping at the open door. "Jessica, put your cap straight, my dear. Abigail, you do us credit, but where is your prayer book? A modest maid goes to her nuptials with the Word of the Lord in her hands."

He looked, she thought resentfully, extremely pleased with himself, and in his own opinion he had every right to be. His pension had been doubled; his fine would be paid; and his daughter was going to her marriage with no dowry.

Temperance and Mercy were in the hall as she passed through. Fresh-faced girls, their hair strained under linen caps, they bobbed curtseys, their eyes full of curiosity. The betrothal of Mistress Abigail to her Royalist cousin had shocked and excited them greatly, but they had not dared to gossip about it. Master Lane was a fair master but a strict one, and any servant stepping out of her place was liable to feel his stick across her back.

Master Penrose, who had been incumbent at the church since the end of the war, greeted them solemnly in the porch. Abigail's betrothal to Paget Delaney had shocked him beyond measure, but Master Lane had not favoured him with any details.

Above his black cassock and starched white neck-bands his long face grew longer as he saw the gleaming topazes and the emerald ring.

There were neither flowers nor music, and the sunshine poured through windows of plain glass into the bare interior. The stained glass, the painted statues, the gilt-fronted altar, all had been swept away years before by the Parliament men.

Jessica, anxiously tugging at her cap, hurried with Master Penrose into the body of the church, and Josiah gripped Abigail's elbow as if he feared she might suddenly take it into her head to run away.

Paget Delaney turned his head as she came slowly up the aisle, and something leaped at the back of his eyes and was stilled as he bowed. Certainly Master Penrose had cause to look affronted. The bridegroom wore a jacket of black velvet over a shirt of embroidered lace, and his full breeches were decorated with loops of purple and silver to match the cockade on his high-crowned black hat. Silver buckles glinted on his shoes and at his hip was a short sword, its hilt ornamented with a turquoise.

At his side a gentleman clad in gold-embroidered blue satin gave Abigail a lengthy, considering glance and raised his eyebrows in an impertinent and startled approval.

The service was not long. She heard Paget make his vows in a lazy, amused drawl and her own small, clear voice answering. The groomsman stepped forward with the ring and the glinting circle was slipped on to her finger. Paget's hand was warm, and for an instant her own cold fingers clung to it and the queer, sick feeling inside her faded a little.

"I now pronounce you man and wife," the minister said, as gloomily as if he had just pronounced the death sentence.

Paget, still holding her hand, bowed briefly to the others, slapped a purse on the altar table and strode down the aisle, his heels ringing on the stone. His servant, Robin, waited outside with the horses, his round face schooled to bland indifference.

"If you would like to come back for a nuncheon?" Jessica was saying.

"We'll eat along the way," Paget said, motioning to Robin to bring the horses nearer. "There are several taverns."

"My daughter has never visited a tavern in her life," Josiah said coldly.

"As my wife she may visit quite a few," Paget returned. "You have not met Master Kenton, I believe? Paul Kenton is a friend of mine."

"The only one who keeps him in good order," Paul

Kenton said, shaking hands cordially. "We met in France five or six years ago and have kept company together since."

He was a slender, fair-haired young man with mischief lurking in his blue eyes. Everything about him spoke of light and gaiety, and Abigail warmed towards him.

"You will write to us?" Jessica said, touching Abigail's cheek nervously with puckered lips.

"Yes. As soon as I'm settled." Abigail returned the embrace. A childish desire to throw herself into her mother's arms and beg to be taken home overcame her, but she could see Paget watching over Jessica's shoulder and the curl of his mobile mouth stiffened her resolve.

"Remember always to walk in the fear of the Lord," Josiah advised.

"Yes, father." She accepted his kiss passively. Then Robin cupped his hands and she was lifted on to the saddle.

"Put your cloak back on and pull up the hood," Jessica fussed. "You will take care, won't you?"

"I'll make certain he doesn't beat her more than once a week," Paul said airily as he sprang to his own mount.

Jessica began to cry weakly, the tears sliding down her cheeks and plopping on to her lace collar. Then the horses moved forward, urged by Robin's cheerful voice, and in a few minutes more a little cloud of dust hid the group outside the porch.

They rode in a silence broken only by Robin's whistling. The servant was apparently in high spirits and once, when Abigail glanced back at him, he lowered an eyelid at her in a way that would have shocked Josiah, but awoke in her the desire to giggle.

"We sleep at the Three Feathers tonight," Paget said. It was the first time he had spoken to her in over an hour, and she jumped slightly.

"A tavern?" She had heard of them spoken of as places of sin, and her voice was apprehensive.

"You will find it very agreeable," Paul assured her. "Not even Parliament was able to abolish taverns."

"They ruined churches though," Paget said. "Did you see that poor desecrated shell just now? Everything beautiful in it swept away, destroyed. Incredible that men should act like brutes."

"A church is a place of worship, not a house of Mammon," Abigail said.

"She echoes her father," Paget remarked, speaking across her as if she were invisible. "There's a fine upstanding Puritan gentleman if ever I met one! He contrived to look quite stricken during the ceremony. Well, he may console himself with the thought that he's not losing a daughter but doubling a pension!"

Abigail's cheeks burned with humiliation as she stared ahead. To hear the shameful bargain discussed before a stranger and a servant was intolerable, and what made it even more painful was that in her heart she agreed with him. Her father, whom she had always respected if not loved, had revealed himself as a hypocrite.

It was mid afternoon when they rode into the cobbled yard of a solid, ivy-covered building set back from the main road. Apart from the brightly painted sign swinging over the door there was nothing to distinguish it from a private dwelling, and the man in shirt sleeves and leather apron who emerged, bowing to them, looked respectable.

"Master Delaney, your rooms are ready and a meal

prepared. Your lady wife will require hot water. I'll have it brought up directly, mistress."

She smiled shyly as he helped her dismount and followed him into a narrow passage and up a flight of stairs to a handsomely furnished bedchamber.

"Your bag arrived, mistress," the man said, indicating a large bag on the floor. "Betsy! Betsy, is that water ready?"

A small maidservant, staggering under the weight of a large jug, came in and poured steaming water into the basin on the table.

"Towels and soap are here, mistress," the landlord indicated. "Come along, Betsy. There's wine to be chilled."

As they withdrew Paget came in, pulling off his short cloak of black and silver.

"We'll eat privately downstairs," he said. "You'll not object if Paul joins us? He's been a good friend to me in the past."

"No, of course not." She had backed away a trifle and the smile on his mouth twisted slightly.

"You'd better take off your cloak," he said, and before she could move away again his hands were pushing back the hood, untying the laces at her throat. The tips of his fingers were cool on her skin and a quiver ran along her nerves.

"The man said my bag had arrived," she said hurriedly. "There must be some mistake, for all my clothes are in the saddle-bags."

"All your old clothes," he corrected. "You cannot wear dull Puritan gowns at Court."

"Court?" She stared at him in dismay. "But I assumed – do you mean Delaney Court?"

"I mean the King's Court, my sweet. On the way to

our home we will spend a night at Whitehall. His Majesty knows I am marrying and gave leave for you to be presented. The dress is for you to wear."

He lifted the bag on to the bed as he spoke, unfastened the buckles, and drew out a froth of yellow silk, the flounces of light brown lace trimmed with cream and yellow rosebuds.

"It's beautiful!" Forgetting her dislike of him, she exclaimed in delight, her brown eyes sparkling. "It's the most beautiful dress I ever saw!"

"I will have others made for you," he said, "We will turn this moth into a butterfly and the whole world will envy me. Will you wash first? You have smears of dust on your face, my love, and though I can appreciate the charms of an urchin girl, it seems a pity to waste the water!"

His eyes were laughing at her again, but without mockery. Without knowing exactly why she felt suddenly light-hearted. "I'll wash first and bequeath you my dusty water," she retorted, and smiled back at him as she turned to the basin.

The water was hot and the soap fragrant. She buried her wet face in the towel, then raised it, flushed and glowing, to meet the smiling grey eyes.

"Lord, but you're a pretty thing!" he said softly, and the towel dropped unheeded to the floor as his arms encircled her and his mouth sought her waiting lips. He kissed her gently at first, then with increasing fervour, his hands moving over the thin silk of her gown. Deep within her a small flame was kindled and leapt to meet an answering fire. "Not now." She whispered the words, her eyes half closed, her lips parted.

"Later then, my sweeting." He blew teasingly into her ear and released her, rolling up his sleeves as he bent over the basin. His forearms were strongly muscled, covered with fine black hair. She averted her eyes in a renewed shyness and began to repack the yellow gown.

"I took the liberty of engaging a maidservant for you," he said, splashing vigorously. "Lettice is a good little soul and will serve you faithfully. She used to work for the Kentons, but Mistress Kenton died a year ago, and when Paul returned from France he found his mother's maid in greatly reduced circumstances."

"Did his mother not go to France too?"

"Mistress Kenton was an invalid and could not have stood the Channel crossing, so Lettice stayed with her and took care of her."

"Then I shall be happy to employ her," Abigail told him.

"Shall we go down to eat, then?" He ran a comb through the black locks that fell to his broad shoulders. The ends of his hair curled damply and there was a trace of soap lather on his cheek. She came forward hesitantly and reached up to dab at it with a corner of the towel. There was an intimacy in the gesture which no longer seemed out of place.

Paul was waiting for them in a small dining room at the end of the lower corridor. They had passed a larger room with sawdust on the floor and an array of jugs and bottles ranged along a flat-topped counter. A couple of men with tankards in their hands were rolling dice and another leaned on the counter engaged in conversation with a young man serving the drinks. It had looked very ordinary and pleasant, not at all like the dens of vice against which Josiah had thundered.

The landlord served them and Abigail had to admit that the meal was excellent. The baked carp was stuffed with mushrooms and the duckling served with a cherry sauce. There was a dish of lettuce and cucumbers and sweet peppers sprinkled with tarragon, a shaped pie filled with minced chicken and almonds, tiny cakes thick with cherries and a custard tart browned in the oven and decorated with peaches. The wine was a sparkling one that stung her nose but left sweetness on the tongue, and she sipped it with relish.

"Has Paget told you we go to Whitehall?" Paul enquired.

"To be presented to the King, yes." She had almost said Charles Stuart but stopped herself in time.

"He is the kindest man one could hope to meet," Paget said, "never vengeful, never malicious."

He spoke with an enthusiasm that infected her with an answering sympathy. Dimly she began to realise how such a devotion could lead a young man into running away from home and turning his back on old loyalties.

"We must drink to him," Paul said, raising his goblet. "To his gracious majesty King Charles the Second. Long life and a happy reign!"

"The King!" Paget echoed.

They both glanced at Abigail and she, with colour deepening, touched the glass to her own lips, murmuring, "The King."

"We shall have you as ardent a Royalist as the rest of us soon," Paget said, and she smiled at him uncertainly.

Leaning back in his chair, his long fingers toying with the stem of his glass, the lean planes of his dark face relaxed, he was an attractive figure. Looking at him from under her lashes she was conscious of a mounting excitement. There were so many facets of this man's nature that she was intrigued each time another was revealed.

"Paget told me about Lettice too," she said, "I will be glad to have her as maidservant."

"That's kind of you," replied Paul. "She is a good soul is Lettice. When I was forced to seek refuge in France with other followers of the King she remained with my lady mother and cared for her until her death. She will serve you well."

"And give you female companionship," Paget added. "Delaney Court is a big estate, several hours' ride from our nearest neighbour."

"I think I can remember it," she said, frowning slightly. "There are yews cut into strange shapes and long dark corridors."

"I was reared among those shapes and passages," he said, and there was a sombre note in his voice. Then he laughed and raised his glass again. "To our marriage, my dear, and our mutual happiness."

"I'll drink to that," Paul declared, bowing towards Abigail. "To tell truth, I'm in a mood to drink to anything now that the King is come into his own again! This will be a merry land when we've swept away the last of Cromwell's rule."

Abigail bit her lip uncomfortably. All her life she had heard Cromwell spoken of as a great man, the saviour of the country. Now he was mentioned with contempt and the values that she had been taught to regard as sacred were set at naught.

"Would you like to go up and rest for a while?" Paget enquired. "I will join you later."

"Thank you," she said gratefully and the two men rose, bowing as she withdrew.

A bag containing her nightgown had been brought upstairs during the meal, the basin emptied and refilled, the bedcovers turned invitingly back. In a very little while Paget would join her there. She had made up her mind to hate him, but his kindness had melted her resolve and she was no longer disposed to struggle against the needs of her own awakening nature.

Slowly, almost dreamily, she unpinned her veiled cap and shook loose her hair, imagining Paget's long fingers untangling the strands. Her tight bodice was hooked up the back, however, and impossible for her to manage unaided. There was no bell visible in the room, and after some futile twisting and turning in a vain attempt to reach the tiny hooks, she opened the door and went softly down the stairs, hoping to see Betsy and enlist her help, but the passage was empty and a burst of masculine laughter from the public room caused her to hesitate.

The door to the small apartment where they had enjoyed their meal was still ajar. It was a little embarrassing but surely natural that she should ask Paget to help her, and her hand lifted to the latch when she heard his voice.

"So there's five hundred sovereigns you owe me, my friend! But I'll take your note of hand."

"You're a mite previous." That was Paul's voice. "The wager's not won yet."

"Do you doubt that it will be? You saw the way she looks at me, her eyes big and adoring, her mouth soft for kissing. The wench is half in love with me already."

"The wager was that you would marry your little Puritan cousin and make her surrender to you blindly, loving you beyond all reason. I've not seen that proved yet."

"Nor ever will!" Abigail flung wide the door and stood trembling on the threshold. "You may retain your note of hand, Master Kenton, for I will never love your friend. I will never even like him or respect him, for he tricked me into this marriage by threats, and then confused me with a pretended kindness."

"Mistress." Paul had risen from the table, his face scarlet.

"As for you!" She whirled about to face Paget who sat, granite calm, with the laughter fled from his eyes. "Are you not rich enough already without cheating more money out of your friends? I was right to distrust you from the beginning, for there is no honour in you! As for loving you blindly, I'll not love you in any fashion, and you may make up your mind to that for I'll not alter mine!"

Sobs were tearing at her throat, and in another moment she would be overwhelmed by them. Turning, she ran down the passage and back to her room, her hair streaming over her shoulders, her face convulsed. She had a vague impression that the landlord had emerged and was staring at her in astonishment. Then she slammed the door and rammed the inside bolt into its socket.

To have been forced into wedlock had been shocking enough, but to have been tricked into almost loving a man who regarded her as no more than part of a cheap wager was an abomination. The kisses to which she had surrendered degraded her now. She shivered with self-disgust, wiping her hand over her lips, while the tears she had held back poured down her face.

If Paget Delaney came now he would need to break down the door, for she'd not unbar it. She would never again allow herself to be so betrayed, and with that final resolve she threw herself, careless of her rumpled skirts, on to the wide bed and wept more bitterly than she had ever wept before.

CHAPTER FOUR

It was dusk of the next day when they approached the great palace of Whitehall where the new monarch was holding his court. It had been a wretched journey despite the sunshine, and even Robin had been affected by the silence and downcast looks of the others. Abigail had fallen asleep at last and woken two or three times in the darkness to the sound of cheerful voices. There had apparently been no need to lock her door, for Paget had not come near. She assumed that he had shared Paul Kenton's room.

Betsy had carried up hot water and then a tray with some breakfast on it, and volunteered the information that the two gentlemen had sat up late carousing. Paul Kenton certainly looked the worse for it, his face puffy, his hand clapped to his head as an ostler raised his voice.

"Even the mice have hobnailed boots on now," he groaned.

"Then stop up your ears," Paget said curtly.

He favoured Abigail with no more than a brief nod as she was helped to the saddle.

She had managed to force down some breakfast and had tidied herself as well as she could, smoothing the dress in which she had slept, pinning her hair back severely and shrouding herself in the russet travelling cloak. There was no trace of the smiling girl who had toasted the King the previous day in her tight lips and averted eyes. On her finger the emerald mocked her unhappiness.

They had stopped at midday at a small, crowded inn where the two gentlemen had gone in to eat their meal, and Robin had brought her some bread and cheese and ale which she had eaten at a table in a small garden at the side. She sensed that the man looked at her with a certain sympathy, and the thought that he might know of his master's wager galled her.

When Paget and his friend came out and remounted, they both seemed in slightly better spirits. As if by common consent they ignored her, addressing only an occasional word to each other as they rode. It was evident that she was being treated as if she were a naughty child, and a spark of anger rekindled in the ashes of her unhappiness.

Yet she could not prevent a stirring of interest as the towers and cupolas and arched gateways of Whitehall came into view. She had never been so near to London, nor seen so many people crowded together before. They were streaming into the maze of courtyards, some mounted, others on foot. She couldn't help staring at them for they were all clad in brilliant colours, hair curled, feathered hats upon their heads. There were ladies among them too, though as she observed their painted lips and low-cut bodices she was not sure if that was the correct word to employ.

"We have lodgings reserved," Paget said, speaking to her directly for the first time. "The King generally sups alone and receives in the Presence Chamber afterwards, so we will have the opportunity for a few words then. I will see you later, Paul."

Dismounted, Abigail stood for a moment in bewilderment with people swirling about her. The constant high-pitched chatter confused her and her back ached after the long hours of riding. At her side Paget said, a touch of impatience in his voice, "If you will take my arm I'll guide you through this. Robin will bring whatever we need for tonight."

Without waiting for an answer he gripped her arm and steered her through the mass of extravagantly clothed people. They made their way with some difficulty along the broad corridors, up flights of marble steps, through antechambers gilded and painted in brilliant colours and furnished with delicate tapestry seats and cabinets filled with china ornaments, cameos set on velvet, and embossed dishes.

Their room was at the end of a long passage, its panelled walls dominated by an immense four-poster bed. As Paget closed the door his glance flew to it and he said, "You ought to sleep well here if your conscience is easy."

"My conscience is perfectly easy," she said coldly. "I think you ought to look to your own, sir."

"How prim of you," he returned. "If my name was Thomas Wellborn it might enchant me, but I fear that priggishness bores me."

"Is it so strange that I should resent being part of a wager?" she demanded. "I was forced to this marriage, as you know, by threats made against my father and my betrothed."

"Both of whom yielded with scarcely a whimper. I thought you might enjoy the novelty of a real man for the first time in your life."

"I count honour among the attributes of a real man," she said bitingly. "So far you have shown none."

"And you, my love, have shown no obedience, which is one of the attributes of a real wife," Paget retorted.

"Wife?" She forced herself to laugh though she had begun to shake. "Wife in name only, Master Delaney. I am still virgin and intend to remain so."

"Brave words!" He clapped his hands softly together and grinned at her unpleasantly. "So you are declaring war on me, are you? A new Civil War between Roundhead and Cavalier, and the result will be the same as it was before, I promise you! No wife will wear breeches in my household, my sweet."

"And no husband will hold the whip-hand over me!" she cried.

"As to that, time will tell," he said. "I see there's water here, not as hot as it was at the Three Feathers, but it will wash away the dirt."

He turned from her and began to strip off his jacket and shirt as calmly as if he were alone. His powerful torso gleamed with sweat and there was a faint, musky smell about him that both alarmed and excited her. She had never seen a half-naked man before and her throat was suddenly dry.

"Pass me the towel," he said, beginning to lather himself. "There's one on the stool there."

She passed it at arm's length and retreated to the corner of the room, her hands clutching her cloak to her.

"I'll need help to get these breeches off," Paget said, towelling himself. "I smell more of horse than of man after so many hours on the road!"

"I'll call Robin," she said in a small voice, and fled into the passage.

The servant appeared so quickly that Abigail suspected him of listening at the door, but he went inside without comment and she was left alone. There was a narrow window just down the corridor and she moved to it and stood looking out into a small garden, though it might as well have been planted with nettles for all the pleasure the roses gave her.

The door opened again and Paget came out, Robin at his heels. He had changed his suit of black purple for one of light brown, its sleeves embroidered in gold, a cloak of gold tissue hanging from one shoulder. Against the creamy ruffles of his shirt his face was darkly handsome, framed in the long black hair.

"My lady wife is a very modest maid," he said, glancing towards his servant. "She is shocked by our Royalist manners, my Robin. The sight of a man undressing fills her with horror. You can go in now, Abigail, and I'll rustle up Lettice to help you get ready."

"I don't want to come," she said, walking past them into the bedchamber. "You pay your respects to the King. I'll stay here and we can ride on to Delaney Court tomorrow."

The door slammed and his hand fell on her shoulder, twisting her around to face him. There was contempt in his expression and his voice cracked like a whip about her ears.

"Whatever you may think of me, whatever you may think of our marriage, you'll not shame me by insulting the King! In public you will behave as becomes a loving and dutiful wife. His Majesty has agreed to meet you, and you will wait upon him at nine o'clock in the Presence Chamber. I will send Lettice to you with something to eat, and when you've eaten, you'll dress yourself in your Court gown, and come to the Presence Chamber, and act as if the only thing in the world you ever wanted was to be presented at the Stuart court."

She opened her mouth to reply furiously but his

mouth fastened upon hers, his teeth biting into her lip, his hands sliding beneath her cloak to crush her against him. Slowly, lingeringly, he explored her with lips and hands evoking a response against which she could not even struggle.

He had released her before her own passion had leaped to full life and she opened her eyes upon his mocking face, the grey eyes brilliant.

"I'll win my wager yet," was all he said, and he was gone before she could collect her wits.

Always he tricked her, winding her in skilfully as a fisherman winds in a fish, playing her as if she were a thing created for his own amusement. And always her own body tricked her, nerves quivering, flesh yearning, waking in her a hunger for something she had never tasted.

Helplessly she clenched her hands, pacing the small chamber like some caged animal. That was very near the truth, she thought bitterly, for she was trapped by her own wanton desire for a man she hated.

There was a tap on the door and she stiffened, her voice high and hard as she called, "Enter."

"If you please, mistress, I am Lettice Andrews." The woman who curtseyed before her was already in her thirties to judge from her face, but her smile was pleasant and her figure slender.

"Oh, yes, of course," Abigail made an effort to collect herself.

"Master Kenton told me that you are willing to engage me," Lettice said. "I'm grateful to you, mistress, for to tell the truth it's been lonely since my late mistress died. I am used to a smaller household than this."

"Have you been to Delaney Court?"

Lettice shook her head. "No, and I'm told it's a big estate, but it cannot possibly be as large as this. I still get confused when I try to find my way about."

"But you know the way to the Presence Chamber?"

"Oh, yes, mistress, though I was never presented to the King myself, of course. Oh, I brought some supper for you. Master Kenton said you'd likely want to eat privately."

She was holding a tray which she set down on the table. There was chicken on it and tiny cold potatoes in a mint-green sauce and an apple tart. Abigail glanced at it without interest and began to untie the strings of her cloak.

"I saw Master Delaney just now," Lettice said. "He's a fine gentleman, mistress. A very kind gentleman, if you'll excuse the liberty, with a great sense of humour. Now, if you'll set your mind to eating, I'll just get some warm water and we'll lay out the dress you're going to wear."

She bustled out and Abigail took up the two-pronged fork and nibbled some chicken. Common sense told her that it was foolish not to eat, but anger still bubbled in her.

"I contrived to get some water," Lettice announced, returning in triumph. "People don't put themselves out to help other people in this place, I can tell you. They're too busy jostling for favours from His Majesty. My, but you look as if you'd slept in this dress! I'll have to clean it as soon as we get to Delaney Court. Turn around so that I can unhook you."

Abigail submitted to the other's ministrations with gratitude. Lettice had a gently soothing voice that ran on like the murmuring of a stream. She would have made a tranquil wife, but apparently she had devoted her youth to caring for a sick woman. Yet she must have been attractive once. Her skin was only faintly pocked and her waist was as small as Abigail's own.

Staring at the maid as she towelled herself dry Abigail's mind began to work rapidly.

"You said that Master Delaney had a sense of humour," she said.

"Yes, indeed he has. The King himself is said to enjoy his wit."

"Then we will please them both," Abigail said, "and show that women too have a sense of humour. Those bags over there contain a couple of dresses."

"I'll get them for you, mistress," Lettice said promptly.

"No, I'll show you my jest!" Pushing aside the tray, Abigail sprang up and hurried to open the bags.

"Mistress, that's a beautiful dress!" Lettice exclaimed as the yellow gown was drawn out.

"And will suit you," Abigail said.

"Suit me?" the maid gasped. "You cannot be serious!"

"Nay, 'tis a jest," Abigail corrected. "I will go to the Presence Chamber in my plainest dress and you will accompany me in Court attire. The King and Master Delaney will be vastly amused."

"I'm sure I don't know," Lettice said doubtfully, but her eyes dwelt lovingly on the yellow silk.

"We'll help each other," Abigail said firmly.

Twenty minutes later they gazed at each other in suppressed amusement. Abigail had donned her black mourning dress, its high neck and long sleeves unrelieved by any touch of colour. Her hair was scraped back tightly under a white linen cap and she had slipped off her betrothal ring.

In contrast Lettice was an elaborate and colourful figure, the yellow dress foaming about her, a yellow ribbon twined through her mousy hair, the topaz necklace glowing above the lace frill of the low-cut neckline.

For an instant Abigail was touched by wistfulness. In the yellow gown she would have looked exquisite, but then her resolution stiffened again. Paget, as her husband, had the right to order her to meet the Stuart King, but she would meet him on her own terms.

"It's nearly nine o'clock, mistress," Lettice said.

"Then we'll go." Abigail drew a deep breath and opened the door.

There was the possibility that he might have waited to escort her, but the corridor was empty, and after a brief hesitation she went boldly forward with Lettice following.

Although it was not yet dark candles blazed in hundreds throughout the palace. There were guards at the doors but they made no effort to stop the groups of people who strolled through the antechambers and courtyards. Servants carrying trays of sweetmeats and pitchers of wine mingled with the gaily dressed courtiers, and in one high gallery musicians played a tune that made Abigail's toes twitch as if her feet had a will of their own and wanted to dance.

"This is the Presence Chamber," Lettice whispered. "We are not allowed beyond this point without permission."

An official in green and gold livery stood at the door, a list of names in his hand which he frequently consulted as a thin stream of people entered the carved and painted chamber beyond.

His look of well-bred astonishment as he beheld Abigail made her quail. Then she clenched her fists against the black skirt, said, "Mistress Abigail Delaney and Lettice Andrews," and swept past him.

There were knots of people standing about and a few elderly ladies occupying chairs and stools ranged along the walls. That much she took in at a glance and then, her knees trembling, she was making her way along a wide red carpet to a low dais on which a tall man, with an ugly mouth and long black ringlets, lounged in a high-backed chair with a small canopy over it.

Paget stepped forward and she glimpsed a flash of primitive, undiluted rage in his face. It was gone directly, to be replaced by a frozen mask in which she could read nothing, and then he had gripped her hand so tightly that she almost cried out with the pain of it, and was bowing.

"Sire, may I present my wife, Abigail?"

The King's heavy-lidded eyes swept over her, rested briefly on Lettice and then returned to her own face. Rising from her curtsy she met the indolent, cynical gaze and felt suddenly mean and small.

"You have an eccentric taste in dress, madam," the King observed.

"My wife is of Puritan stock, sire," Paget said.

"And does not scruple to display the fact," Charles Stuart said.

"I am not ashamed of my beliefs," Abigail affirmed. She had meant the sentence to sound firm and fearless, but it came out quaveringly. Somewhere in the room someone tittered.

"She is honest, sire, and that is a rare commodity at Court," Paget interposed.

"So is horse-dung, but we do not bring that into the Presence Chamber," said a lady seated near the King.

She was a handsome green-eyed woman with red hair

piled on her head, and a gown cut so indecently low that Abigail wondered how she had dared appear in public.

"Barbara, my love, you always have the apt phrase for the right moment," the King observed, his heavy face breaking into a lazy and undeniably attractive smile.

"And this is –?" He had turned back to Lettice and was beckoning her forward with a beringed hand.

"Lettice Andrews, sire. I am maid to Mistress Delaney." Her voice shook.

"I see you do not object to wearing pretty dresses," he remarked.

"No, sire."

"Then you will not object to taking a glass of wine with a Stuart?"

"No, sire."

Charles made a slight, languid gesture and two footmen approached with a decanter and goblets.

Abigail stood for a moment, her face crimsoning, as Lettice stepped forward shyly to accept a glass. The King, inclining his head slightly in Paget's direction, said pleasantly, "I wish you joy of your marriage, Delaney. You will attend me next month? I intend to review the Fleet and hold some water banquets."

"Your Majesty honours me," Paget said. His face was still set in grimly unrelenting lines, but he offered Abigail his arm with perfect courtesy.

"Will you dance? They are forming a set," he enquired.

"I – cannot. I don't know the steps," she faltered.

"Then you will excuse me if I find a more willing partner?" Releasing her, he bowed gracefully and moved away. A few moments later she saw him lead the red-haired woman out on the floor.

The King was giving Lettice his hand to kiss, saying something that evidently amused her, for she was smiling as if she were quite at her ease.

"Wine, mistress?" One of the servants had paused before her.

"Yes, thank you." She took a glass and gulped the liquid within, choking slightly for it was a full-bodied Madeira such as they never had at home. The room tilted slightly, then settled back into its rightful place.

More people were dancing now, treading a complicated measure, the flowing skirts of the ladies whispering over the floor, the gentlemen's heels tapping out the rhythm. Abigail backed to the wall and stood there, the glass still in her hand, her eyes watering as she fought against dizziness. One or two people glanced at her curiously but nobody spoke or smiled. She had the feeling that she had become, not invisible, but of such small account that she would be ignored for the rest of her life.

Putting the glass down on a table she took a last, miserable look round the brilliant assembly and made her way to the door. Beyond the Presence Chamber people still strolled and chatted. There were corridors leading off in all directions and she tried desperately to remember which way they had come.

"Mistress Abigail?" Lettice hurried up to her. "Do you want to go back to your room?"

"If you're not too busy supping wine with the King," Abigail said sharply, and then put out her hand, speaking in quick apology. "Forgive me, but I am in an evil humour and my head aches. You'd better show me the way to my room, and then you'll be free to do as you please for the rest of the evening."

"Oh, I shall retire and get a good night's sleep before

we leave tomorrow," Lettice said. "I am very grateful to you for taking me into your service, mistress, and for allowing me to wear this dress. I know it was a jest but, just for a little while, I felt like a real lady."

"A sour jest," Abigail muttered and cast a brooding look at the wedding ring on her finger.

They reached the bedchamber without mishap and changed their gowns in silence. Lettice, after a furtive glance at her mistress's face, had the tact not to attempt any further conversation, and contented herself with a respectful, "Goodnight, mistress," as she withdrew.

Candles had been lit in the room and were reflected in the small panes of the window. Between them she could discern her own face, a pale disc floating above the gloom of a deepening twilight.

Abruptly she put her hands to her face and shivered, shame burning through her. Anger had betrayed her into a course of action that now seemed to her to be stupid and ill-mannered. It was not Paget who had been humiliated but herself. Even Lettice had been offered the privilege of a glass of wine with the King. Worst of all had been the cold fury in Paget's face when he saw her Puritan garments. She would not easily forget that look or the contempt in his grey eyes.

It was not what she had intended. Her defiance had been designed to make him realise that she was not willing to compromise her own principles. All that she had succeeded in doing was making him despise her, and with a cruel and blinding clarity she knew that was the last opinion of her she wanted him to hold.

There was no use her denying any longer that she desired the husband she had been forced to marry. His beliefs were not hers, and his arrogant manners roused her to fury, but the touch of his hand awoke in her a wanton need that she had been taught was sinful. Perhaps, in that at least, Josiah was wrong. That he might be wrong in other matters was something else she was not yet prepared to consider.

There might still be time to repair a little of the harm she had done. She snatched up the yellow dress and struggled into it. It fastened at the side, a circumstance for which she was heartily thankful, and it fitted her more smoothly than it had fitted Lettice, the lace ruffles emphasising her high breasts and foaming about her ankles.

Impatiently she unclipped her hair and shook it loose. There was no time to curl it, but she pulled a yellow ribbon from the trimmings of the gown and tied back two side wings of the gleaming brown mass.

She could enquire the way back to the Presence Chamber and pray that her reappearance in Court dress would mitigate the bad impression she had created.

Taking a deep breath she opened the door and came face to face with Paget, his own hand almost on the latch.

"So?" As she drew back he stepped within the room, his thin brows raised as he stared at her.

"I was – returning," she stammered.

"To the Presence Chamber? The King took the backstairs with Barbara Palmer a while since, and is not receiving again."

"With the lady who danced with you?"

"The King's mistress," he nodded. "She condoled with me on my choice of wife."

"The King's mistress?" she echoed faintly. "His Majesty has a—"

"You must have been reared in complete ignorance," he said coldly. "Of course the King has a mistress. He is thirty years old and unmarried. Do you think he spends all his time on his knees in chapel?"

"We could still return," she said, reverting to the original subject. "It isn't very late."

"A great deal too late," he said, "I don't care to watch my wife make a fool of herself twice."

"Paget!" The cry broke from her imploringly as she clutched his sleeve. "I didn't mean – I altered my mind."

"In the space of thirty minutes? You're more weather-cock than wife!"

"I am not yet wife, save in name," she reminded him.

"So you begin to realise that, do you?" He shook her free, not violently but as if she were an importunate child. "Is that why you rushed back to change? Did you really think I would be tempted by a few bits of lace and a more – extensive view of your undeniably seductive body? If I want you, my loving wife, I'll take you and enjoy you whether you're in bright plumage or clad in a sack!"

His voice mocked her but there was a throbbing note in it which sent shivers crawling down her spine. She moved nearer, her eyes raised to his, her lips parted for the embrace that would crush her into surrender.

"However," said Paget, his voice slowing into a drawl, "I have decided that you're not worth the trouble, so I'll bid you goodnight, mistress."

His words struck her like a blow, and as she reeled under the pain of them, he bowed and went out, closing the door with insulting gentleness.

CHAPTER FIVE

LETTICE woke her early the next morning with a tray of food and the information that it was raining.

"So you'll need to wrap up, mistress, for the roads can be knee-deep in mud in a matter of hours if it doesn't clear up," she advised. "Master Delaney says that he will meet us in the courtyard."

"He was not much amused by my jest," Abigail said.

"I thought not, but the King was most gracious to me," Lettice said. "I felt quite at my ease after a few minutes. But I'm sorry that it should cause trouble."

"It makes no matter." Abigail shrugged and applied herself to her breakfast.

She was dressed and fastening her cloak when a tap on the door announced Robin, who had come for the bags. The servant gave his usual cheerful greeting, but the look he bestowed on her was one of frank curiosity.

There seemed to be almost as many people wandering about in the halls and corridors as there had been the previous night. As she and Lettice followed Robin, Paul Kenton broke away from a group of gentlemen and drew her aside. "We didn't meet last evening, Mistress Abigail," he began. "I was not bidden to the Presence Chamber, and Paget said you left early with a headache."

"We had a quarrel," she said flatly.

"I thought it might have been that." His pleasant face was troubled. "I do regret what happened at the inn. It was – a foolish wager, made when we were both in our cups. At the time we neither of us had any money at all nor expected to have any, and then the King was recalled, and we returned with him. My mother had left sufficient for me to live comfortably, and then Paget's father died."

"And he kept the wager. He married his Puritan cousin, but as to the rest—" Her voice was toneless. "As to the rest, Master Kenton, your money is safe. I have no affection for my husband and never will have."

He would have detained her longer, but she bowed coldly and walked on, with Lettice following her meekly.

Paget was already mounted, figure and features shrouded in cloak and broad-brimmed hat. Robin helped Abigail and Lettice to their own horses, and they clattered out of the yard into the drizzling rain.

"We strike west through the royal parks," Paget said over his shoulder. "We'll ride as fast as possible without overtiring the horses. Then we can reach Delaney Court in good time for luncheon."

She nodded, her eyes averted, and he hunched himself into the saddle again and rode on through the dripping trees. Abigail began to regret Paul's absence for he, at least, had been cheerful company, but Lettice had mentioned that he would be remaining in his bachelor lodgings at Whitehall

The rain eased as they rode through the spacious parks, and a faint sun made the wet leaves seem to glint and dance. At any other time Abigail would have enjoyed the ride but, with Paget's unyielding back before her eyes, she felt her spirits sink as the miles increased.

Delaney Court, she knew, was not in the town of Windsor but a few miles distant, on land granted to the Delaneys more than a hundred years before. Jessica had hinted once or twice that her brother considered she had married beneath her and, apart from an occasional visit, relations between the two families had never been very cordial.

They had entered the forest now and the interlacing branches overhead repelled the sunlight. "There is good hunting here," Robin said.

His voice echoed queerly in the mossy glade, and she glimpsed the scut of a coney bob among the tall grass that bordered the mossy path. They came out of the trees on to a wider track and Paget gestured to open gates ahead of them.

"The estate begins here," he said. Abigail had a dim memory of the long drive curving between gigantic oaks to lawns set about with yews carved into peacocks and dragons. She had expected that the house might appear smaller than it had seemed when she was a child, but its stone facade reared up before her as they approached, dwarfing both riders and horses.

It was a three-storey building with wings jutting back and rows of narrow windows set deep into the mullions with leering gargoyles jutting out above them. A flight of shallow steps led up to the massive oak door and Abigail stared up at it apprehensively as she dismounted.

"Welcome home, my dear wife," Paget said. His smile was ironical as he took her arm and began to ascend the steps.

As they reached the door it was opened from within

and they stepped into a stone-floored hall with a staircase twisting up to a gallery above. Against the walls dark tapestries hung motionless and, though it was high summer and the rain had ceased, the place was cold and dim.

"Do you remember this?" Paget asked her.

She shook her head, her eyes moving slowly round the vast apartment. "Only the yew, and long passages with portraits hanging on the walls," she said uncertainly.

"That would be upstairs. My father spent most of his time in his rooms."

"And your mother?"

"She died when I was six years old," he said briefly. "No, don't bother to say you're sorry. The poor woman was glad to die, I imagine, with such a husband!"

Abigail gave him a startled look as they began to mount the stairs. He had spoken out, not apparently caring that there were servants in the hall and that Lettice was following.

From the gallery passages led off to left and right, dark narrow corridors hung with framed portraits and so dim that she began to feel that the walls were closing in on her.

"This is the master bedroom," Paget said. "My father used one of the rooms on the upper floor. Lettice, go downstairs and tell Robin to make you known to the rest of the household. Your mistress will require you later, I've no doubt."

Lettice bobbed a curtsy and withdrew. Abigail drew away from Paget's grasp and walked over to one of the windows. It looked out over the curving drive, the green lawns and darker green of the yews and beyond to where the forest began.

"I will take the room down the passage, if that meets with your approval," his voice said in a tone of cool politeness.

Without turning she said with equal coolness, "You must please yourself. It makes no difference to me."

"And this apartment will suit you?"

"Very well." Her heart sank a little more as she turned and gazed round. Her bedchamber at Lane House had been only a slip of a room opening off the one her parents shared, and it had been simply furnished. This apartment was tapestry-hung in rich shades of crimson, pale blue and gold, and there were carpets on the floor. She feared that even with the candles lit and a fire blazing in the wide hearth she would still be lonely.

"My father used the rooms above these," Paget said. "I suppose that he liked to be as near to Heaven as possible, so that he could the better pretend that he was God. There is a dressing room next door to this with a hip bath in it, so you can be as clean as you please. Robin will have your things brought up. You can eat some luncheon here if you like and we'll meet at supper. I have estate business to manage, but you may go wherever you choose, of course."

He bowed and went out again, without having tried to touch her, without even a smile.

A few minutes later Robin came in with the bags. Abigail was not sure she approved of the manservant's inquisitive looks but she could not resist saying, as he put them down, "Have you been with Master Delaney for a long time?"

"About two years, ever since my late master died in France. We had a very hard time of it but Master Delaney never gave up hope of the King's being recalled. He took me into service and said he'd pay me when he came back to his father's estate," Robin said.

"Did you ever meet Master Henry Delaney?" she ventured.

"No, mistress. When we first landed everybody went at once to the Court, and when Master Delaney came here his father was already dying."

"And so the estate came to Paget."

"Oh, it was a gloomier place than it is now," he said, "but Master Delaney had this apartment specially redecorated for you, mistress. He is going to have the whole house done, but this chamber had to be beautiful for his wife, he said."

"I see. Thank you, Robin. That will be all."

So the room had been designed for her pleasure. In that, at least, he had displayed consideration. Glancing at the wide bed with its hangings of pale blue and gold, she wondered if he had had their mutual pleasure in mind.

A bitter little smile twisted her mouth and she shivered, for Paget had made it clear that she would occupy this chamber alone, and wake alone in the beautiful bed.

"Shall I help you to change your dress, mistress?" Lettice had put her head round the door and smiled at her.

"I'll wear the russet gown. It's in one of the bags. Have you been given your own room?"

"A few doors down the passage, mistress. This is a very big house, much bigger than the Kenton home was. Master Paul sent word from France when his mother died that his home was to be sold. The steward and I contrived to save the proceeds of the sale against Master Paul's return. Many Cavaliers came back with no money at all," Lettice said, beginning to unpack. "The other servants here seem friendly, mistress. One of them told me that their late master was a harsh man, and they had always been Royalist at heart."

"I imagine a lot of people will be saying that now," Abigail said, taking off her cloak. "They will bend with the wind and be untrue to their beliefs."

"One cannot blame them, mistress," Lettice said, "it is never easy to hold to one's beliefs."

"*You* did, when you stayed to take care of Master Kenton's mother."

"Not so, mistress," Lettice said, beginning to unhook Abigail's dress. "We had to live under the Parliament, and that meant putting away bright colours and singing and dancing. It was safer so. It was not wise then to appear with curled hair and pretty gowns."

"And now it is not wise to dress soberly! Is that what you're saying?" Abigail pulled the folds of the russet gown over her hips.

"It's my belief that it's what is in the heart that counts," the maid said. "Master Delaney has a good heart, mistress, even if his ways are not your ways."

"I don't need anyone to defend my husband to me," Abigail said irritably. "And I'm capable of doing my own hair too, thank you. Go and see if you can find anything to eat in this place and bring me something."

"Yes, mistress," Lettice said meekly. Abigail bit her lip in vexation as the older woman went out. Jessica had always impressed on her that servants were to be kindly treated. She would not have been pleased by her daughter's sharp tongue.

In a little while Lettice returned with baked fish, a salad and some stewed pears in cream.

"The other servants have laid a place for me in the

kitchen with them, mistress," she explained. "They say their late master took his meals alone, but that there were prayers at eight o'clock every evening."

"Then there will be prayers tonight," Abigail decided.

"Yes, mistress." Lettice set down the meal and went away again.

When she had eaten Abigail opened her bedroom door and went out into the long corridor. Paget had said that she might explore and if this was to be her home, then the sooner she became acquainted with it the better. Yet it was with a sense of intrusion that she went from room to room, and she had the uneasy feeling that at any moment she might turn a corner and bump into Uncle Henry Delaney. Apart from the newly decorated bedchamber the rest of the house bore the imprint of his harsh, dark personality. The heavy panelling, the faded tapestries, the carved furniture of oak and ebony oppressed her spirits. This was a building where gaiety and warmth had never entered, and she wondered suddenly how a child must have felt in these sunless corridors. Perhaps Paget had had some excuse for rebellion.

She had just mounted a stair, and opened a door into a long chamber shrouded in dust sheets and with the shutters closed. The room, like all the others, was chilly, but she was curious about the covered furniture and so went briskly to wrestle with the fastenings and open the casements. Under the dust sheets as she tugged them loose were bed, couch, chests embossed in silver and filled with garments of delicately embroidered brocade and jewel-coloured velvet, boxes in which gilt ornaments, feather fans and ivory-backed combs and brushes were jumbled together, a case containing books and sewing materials, and a dainty spinet.

"My mother's things," said Paget from the door. "She loved pretty things about her, but little by little my father made her give them up. When she died everything was stored here. The moth will have got into some of it, I've no doubt."

"What a shame!" She spoke sincerely, but when she spoke again it was in the usual mocking manner.

"A shame indeed! One might have sold the lot and provided the entire county with prayer books instead. The servants tell me that you intend to have prayers at eight o'clock tonight, as it was in my father's time."

"Prayers are customary in every Christian household," Abigail said.

"And you may have yours, naturally."

"You will attend?" She looked at him in sudden misgiving. "The master of the household always conducts the prayers."

"Then we'll bow to convention," he told her.

"I wanted to thank you," she rushed on, "for making the bedchamber so lovely. Robin told me you'd had it redecorated."

"In haste, but I trust the colours please you?"

"Oh, yes. I like pretty colours," she said earnestly. "You must not think because I dress soberly that I cannot appreciate fine things. These ought to be used, not hidden away."

"Then use them by all means," he said. "There are some fine pieces of silver, too. My father hoarded them in his chests, but they can be displayed again. I leave it to you, my dear."

"But won't you –?" She hesitated.

"I return to Court tomorrow," Paget told her. "His

Majesty invited me to attend him when he reviews the Fleet."

"But that isn't until next month," she protested.

"I have other business to see about," he said. "You don't object to my leaving home again, do you?"

"It makes no difference to me whether you go or stay," she said, drawing herself up a little.

"So we have found something on which we agree!" he exclaimed. "I begin to think that this marriage may yet be a success. Have you seen over the entire house?"

"Most of it, but it's confusing."

"Only for strangers." He held the door open for her to pass through. "If you'll do me the favour of coming to the parlour, I want you to meet my steward. John Bailey is a good man, for all that he served my father."

"But he's a Royalist now, I suppose?" she said lightly.

"He does his work well," Paget said briefly, "so I don't enquire into his private convictions."

The parlour had a more cheerful aspect than the hall, a bright fire of applewood logs burning on the hearth, the candles already lit, for a glance through the window revealed that the sun had given up the unequal struggle against the rain and the skies were black.

A soberly clad gentleman in a periwig was bending over some documents on a table, but he straightened up as Abigail and Paget came in.

"John, I told you that you would have the pleasure of meeting my wife," Paget began.

"Indeed you did, Master Delaney." John Bailey bowed over her head. "Welcome to Delaney Court, Mistress Abigail. You won't remember me at all, but we met when you visited with your parents. You were only a little girl then. A very solemn little girl."

"In that respect she has not altered," Paget said. "Will you take a glass of wine with us, John?"

"That's very civil of you, Master Delaney," the steward said, holding out a chair for Abigail. "It will be a pleasure to drink to your happiness. I trust your lady mother is in good health? Mistress Jessica was always a very sweet-natured lady."

"Too sweet-natured to get on well with my late father," Paget said, handing round the glasses.

"The late Master Delaney was not always easy to get on with," John Bailey admitted.

"He was a brute," Paget said. "I can remember his satisfaction when I was a boy and did something which deserved punishment. It pleased him enormously to discover that people were as sinful as he believed them to be."

There was an uncomfortable little silence. Then John Bailey cleared his throat and said, "Master Delaney tells me that he has to return to Court. I hope you will feel able to call upon me, mistress, if you need anything. This is a large estate, but I can make leisure to ride with you one day, and give you some idea of the work we do here."

"That's very kind of you," she responded, sipping her wine.

"Your lady mother used to enjoy riding when she was a girl," the steward said. "Often, when she had a falling out with her brother, Mistress Jessica would saddle her pony and gallop into the woods. I beg your pardon, but I happened to recall that – tactlessly, I fear."

"My aunt was a gentle soul," Paget said. "She married Josiah Lane to get away from home, I believe, and he turned out to be as cheerless as my father. Ironic, isn't it?"

"My father is a very worthy man," Abigail said, bright spots of colour flaming in her cheeks.

"A most sincere Puritan," Paget agreed. "If you've finished exchanging family reminiscences, perhaps we can get back to work, John? You were telling me that some repairs are required to one of the ceilings in the east wing."

"A damp patch," John Bailey nodded. "It ought to be attended to before the winter comes."

"If you'll excuse me—" Abigail began.

"My congratulations to you both, mistress." John Bailey raised his glass to them.

"I've invited John to join us for supper," Paget said. "I thought you might enjoy a little company."

"Yes, of course. It was nice to meet you again, Master Bailey." She bowed slightly as Paget opened the door for her.

"You will change for supper?" he enquired in a low voice as they went into the hall.

"I did change my dress," she said coldly. "I see no need to prink every night as if we were at Court when we are in our own home."

"Simplicity being the keynote in a good Christian family? As you please, my lady wife." He bowed and went back into the other room, closing the door firmly as if he were closing her out of his life.

Angrily she looked down at her russet skirt and modest, white collared bodice. It seemed that nothing she did contented him. When she wore the yellow silk he rejected her, and when she put on her ordinary, everyday gown he suggested that she change it.

The great hall, after the warmth of the parlour, was cheerless. The candles had not been lit yet and the huge fireplace yawned emptily beyond the staircase. Screens at the far end of the hall divided the buttery from the main house. She had not yet been to the kitchens or the servants' quarters, and she went briskly over the flagstones.

The kitchen was much bigger than the one at home in Lane house. She paused on its threshold, bewildered by the chatter and heat from the fires. A trio of maidservants were giggling in one corner and she heard one of them say, "Lord, but she's dressed as plain as plain. Not a curl about her."

"The old master would have approved," another said.

"But I cannot understand what Master Paget sees in her," the third puzzled. "I always thought he would bring back a very dashing young lady, not a little mouse."

There was a small copper hand-bell hanging against the wall. Abigail rang it sharply and there was a sudden stop to the chatter. It seemed that at least twenty pairs of eyes were turned in her direction as she came further into the steamy room.

"I don't know all your names yet," Abigail said, raising her voice nervously, "but I shall learn them soon, and your duties. Of one thing, however, I am certain already. Your duties do not consist of gossiping about your betters. There is supper to be prepared."

"It's all cooking, mistress." A plump, elderly woman hurried forward, wiping floury hands on her apron. "Two plump ducks and a chine of beef and some almond cake. Is the supper to be in the solar, or in the hall?"

"The solar, if you please," Abigail decided. "Master Bailey will be joining us."

"Yes, mistress, Master Paget did tell us."

"And prayers will be at eight o'clock," Abigail said firmly. "I shall expect all of you to be present. That's all."

She nodded briefly, aware of their staring eyes and the half-stifled giggle of one of the maids. Perhaps it had been a mistake to let them know she had overheard their remarks. It might have been more dignified to have ignored them. As she left the kitchen the chatter broke out again in more subdued fashion, and she feared it was not very complimentary to the master's new wife.

CHAPTER SIX

THE evening went off more smoothly than Abigail had expected. Paget gave her russet gown one brief, meaning look but made no audible comment. John Bailey set himself to be friendly and talkative, amusing her with tales of her mother as a young girl. Jessica, after the elder Delaneys had died, had been reared by her brother and had often flouted his authority. Abigail, remembering her mother's gaiety when Josiah was away at the war, thought it a pity she had married a man so like Henry Delaney in character.

The household had assembled for prayers and Paget, his face without expression, had read one of the psalms and then embarked on what Abigail considered to be an unnecessarily lengthy discourse on the blessings of having a monarchy again. But the servants had listened with apparent interest, and their fervent Amens had drowned her more muted response.

A fire had been lit in her room and candles blazed, but although Abigail waited for almost an hour Paget did not come near. He had bidden her a cool goodnight in the hall, his lips brushing her cheek, and gone with the steward to give some final instructions about the estate. She had half-expected a more private goodnight, but there was no knock on her door, and she fell asleep at last with the glow of the fire to dispel the shadows.

Lettice roused her in the morning with a breakfast tray and the news that Master Paget had ridden out with Robin and would return when his business was completed.

"And Master Bailey says that if you wish to go riding he is at your service."

"Does Master Bailey live in the house then?" Abigail asked.

"No, mistress. I understand that he has a small house on the estate," Lettice told her.

A ride would refresh her spirits, Abigail decided. She ate her breakfast and then dressed, putting on the russet again and covering it with her travelling cloak. The rain of the previous day had ceased and when she went out into the open the lawns shimmered as green as the emerald on her hand.

John Bailey was waiting for her with two saddled horses. "Cora is my own mount," he said as he greeted her, "but she is more suited to a lady than a gentleman. I hope you will accept her as a token of my good wishes."

"That's very kind of you. She can be stable mate to my own pony." Abigail stroked the mare's glossy flanks and allowed the steward to help her to the saddle.

"I thought you might enjoy an excursion to the village," John Bailey said. "It's no more than a mile distant and most of the people who live there work on the estate. They will be eager to meet the new mistress."

'Who was married for the sake of a wager and now desires the husband who despises her', Abigail thought, but she merely nodded and smiled as they trotted between the shaped yews.

Beyond the formal gardens stretched meadows and copses of dark trees. There were cattle placidly grazing and fields of ripening corn were visible over the tangled hedges. Abigail's depression lifted a little as they rode. She was after all young and healthy and, if necessary, she would fight for her rights as a wife. It was a sour jest that she had begun by swearing she would never submit and now was planning ways to attract her husband back again!

The village was no more than a cluster of cottages in a hamlet, within the centre a patch of green on which stood a tall pole hung with long coloured ribbons.

"The villagers put it up to celebrate the King's return," John Bailey pointed.

"Is it a maypole?" She had no memory of ever having seen one, but she had often heard Josiah fulminate against the evils of them.

"Forbidden under the Parliament," he nodded. "It was said to be a lewd pagan relic around which simple folk danced in honour of the ancient fertility gods."

"But didn't Paget's father object?"

"He was never aware it had been put up, being already on his deathbed."

"And you didn't tell him? Are you then a King's man at heart?"

"I am my own man, mistress," he returned with dignity. "To tell the truth, I never saw any harm in a little merriment. If you will dismount then I will introduce some of the villagers to you."

She dismounted and allowed him to lead her over the cobbles to where a few people had gathered to watch them. As John Bailey introduced them she could see the curiosity in their faces. She could sense too a certain disappointment as they saw her unadorned garments, although they greeted her with respect, wishing her happiness. She noticed that the cottages appeared to be in good repair and the people looked healthy and decently clothed. Her uncle, for all his harsh ways, had evidently been a fair master.

"Mistress Abigail, my own house is not far distant from here," John Bailey said when they were remounted. "It would be an honour if you would call in with me."

She accepted, waved her hand to the knot of villagers who looked as if they could hardly wait for her to depart so that they could begin talking again, and rode on with him, away from the tiny village and through a woodland trail which brought them to a fair-sized lodge.

"My father was steward here before me," John Bailey told her as he helped her down, "he and my mother served your grandparents as I now serve Master Paget."

There was a small but charming garden and an orchard at the side, which reminded her so strongly of home that her eyes pricked with tears.

Within the house a narrow parlour opened out of a modest hall and a maidservant brought in some wine and cake as they settled themselves there.

"Meg and her husband attend to my needs," John Bailey said, smiling at the woman as she bobbed a curtsy and went out.

"You don't have a wife then?" Abigail questioned as she took the proffered glass.

"No, I never married." He spoke briefly and for a moment she thought he intended to change the subject, but he went on, his voice musing. "I suppose it will hurt nobody now if I tell you that when I was a young man I had a great admiration for your lady mother. Mistress

Jessica was one of the comeliest maids I ever saw."

"You and my lady mother?" Glass halfway to her lips, she stared at him.

"No, mistress. It would not have been fitting for me to speak of it to her," he said. "Master Henry Delaney would have turned me off at the barest hint of it. He had just wed himself and Master Paget was a babe. Mistress Jessica used to ride over sometimes to pass the time of day. She regarded me as a friend, you see, and sometimes she'd confide in me. She always believed that her brother meant her to stay unwed so that he'd not need to pay her dowry, and I remember how she vowed that she would be married in spite of him. The master couldn't make a valid objection when she chose Josiah Lane, for he was a steady Puritan, but he was not pleased, and she came back only once after that, when you were a small girl."

"And you never married?"

"No, mistress. I never met a woman for whom I cared sufficiently," he told her.

"I'm sorry," Abigail said gently.

"Oh, I'm pretty well content," he said. "I have this house and garden and my work, and I'm a great reader. I subscribe to a London newsletter and, when I have time to spare, I ride to Oxford or to London itself and buy books. I have gone through Raleigh's *History of The World* two or three times already, and it still amazes me."

"I would like to travel," Abigail said. "I used to watch the river flowing past the end of our garden sometimes and wish I could sail on and on, to find out where it led."

"It's likely that Master Paget will take you visiting when he returns," the steward said. "It's a pity he had to rush away so quickly, but he knows the estate is in good hands."

"Very good hands," she complimented.

John Bailey looked pleased. "I do what lies in my power," he said modestly. "The old master trusted me for he was something of a recluse, you know, especially after Master Paget ran away to join the King."

"Which was most undutiful of him," she could not resist saying.

"He had a hard boyhood," the steward said. "After the mistress died Master Delaney turned the lad over to tutors, and drummed the Bible into his ears day in and day out. The war was on and Master Paget was red-hot for the King. In the end he ran away, though by then it was a lost cause, for everyone knew that the King's party would lose."

"And now the monarchy is restored," she said thoughtfully.

"And I cover my cropped hair with a periwig." He glanced at her shyly and then said, "You must forgive my bluntness, mistress, but I could not help noticing that you still wear Puritan garb. It's my belief that you would find life easier if you compromised a little."

"I cannot deck myself like a peacock when I have been taught to despise worldly vanity," she said, and thought how priggish she must sound.

"Of course not, mistress." He spoke respectfully, but she fancied he looked a little disappointed. When he spoke again, however, his voice was as pleasantly cheerful as before.

"I fancy you'll not have had much experience of managing a large household, mistress, but it will come easy to you in a short time. The late master insisted that all his servants performed their work diligently, and the outdoor staff are under my own jurisdiction, but you will come to me if you require help, I trust?"

"Most willingly," she said promptly, rising and smiling at him.

So far she didn't seem to have made such a good impression on the people she had met, and it would be comforting to have a friend in the quiet man who had had such an affection for her mother.

There was certainly much to occupy her time in the days and weeks which followed. Like most girls, Abigail had been taught to sew and bake and infuse cordials and tisanes from the herbs that grew wild around the countryside, but Lane House had been a modest property. At Delaney Court ten servants were employed in the house and a further forty worked the land. Apart from baking and brewing, there were the stewponds to be stocked, the first crops of apples and pears to be stored, pigs and poultry to be slaughtered and salted, butter to be churned, soap and candles to be made, linen to be sorted for its annual wash, tapestries to mend, bulbs to be lifted and new plants laid down, and materials to be ordered from the pedlar when he came round with his samples.

From the moment she emerged from her room in the morning until the household gathered for prayers in the evening, Abigail was busy, moving from hall to kitchen and back again, hurrying into the garden to give her opinion on where a particular shrub ought to be planted, or to the stables to approve the bran feed that the groom had mixed.

In one way she was grateful for the ceaseless activity, for it afforded her no leisure in which to brood over Paget's continued absence or his silence. Not a single letter had come for her since his departure, and there were moments when she feared that he intended to remain at Court for ever and leave her neglected in the big, gloomy house.

She ventured up to the top floor on one occasion and wandered through the rooms where Uncle Henry Delaney had spent so much of his solitary life. The chambers were low-ceilinged, opening out of one another, with narrow windows set so low that one had to bend to catch a glimpse of the grounds below.

Rush matting on the oaken floor, dark tapestries and iron candlesticks imparted an air of austerity to the rooms, an air intensified by the furniture carved with the same gargoyle faces that decorated the outside of the house. There was nothing in this part of Delaney Court to remind one of the loveliness of summer or the beauties of nature. Abigail had never been in such dark, gloomy surroundings before, and she shivered inwardly as she went from room to room seeing, in her mind's eye, the tall, forbidding figure of Uncle Henry Delaney.

Perhaps Paget stayed away because he could not endure the memories these rooms conjured up. It could not have been pleasant to grow up in these sombre surroundings. Her own home had been comfortable and cheerful despite Josiah's strictness, and her sympathy for the boy that Paget had been grew stronger. It would surely do no harm to brighten the rest of the house a little? She would have the dark hangings replaced by lighter ones, fires and more candles lit in every room, and great armfuls of blossom to splash colour into the shadowy corners. When Paget did return it would be to a warmer, brighter dwelling place.

John Bailey, to whom she confided her scheme, was enthusiastic. "Delaney Court is a handsome dwelling place, mistress," he said, "and it could be made into a beautiful one with a little imagination. The main wing is Tudor, and I've often thought it a shame to cover up all that lovely old wood with those dismal tapestries."

"It won't cost a great deal," she began, but he held up his hand.

"Master Delaney died a wealthy man, for he spent little and invested wisely. I have access to whatever is needed for the payment of wages and the upkeep of the estate, so you order what you require and I'll see it's bought. We've got to make haste, though, if it's to be done in a fortnight."

"A fortnight?" She gave him a questioning glance.

"For when Master Paget comes home." His own expression was one of surprise. "He wrote yesterday, warning me to expect him."

"I had forgotten," she said quickly, too proud to admit that she had received no word. "However, if we make a start in the great hall then we can do the rest little by little."

"And I am certain there will be a transformation," he said. "You know, both Mistress Jessica and Master Paget's lady mother tried to bring a touch of elegance to Delaney Court, but the master was against any idle luxuries, as he called them."

"He does sound exceedingly unpleasant," she admitted.

"He was a man of narrow views and unassailable conscience," John Bailey said. "There was nothing dishonest in his nature, and he stuck close to his principles. I always admired him for that."

'As I stick to mine,' Abigail thought, 'but Paget doesn't admire me at all.'

She took leave of the steward and went out into his

garden, where Cora waited patiently beyond the wall. So Paget was coming home in two weeks. The hurt she felt at his not having written was mitigated by excitement. Surely he would be pleased by the changes she intended to make, and the coolness between them warm into friendship at least.

Despite her duties she had contrived to take a short ride or walk every day. It was a relief to be out in the fields and woods away from the dim rooms, where her footsteps echoed and the sound of her own breathing was loud in her ears. The only convivial place was the big steamy kitchen but, when she entered it, the servants became quiet and respectful, their eyes telling her quite clearly that she was not really welcome. Even Lettice was not much assistance, for all her talk was of how kind Master Paget was.

"You see Master Paul, being still unwed and not having settled into his own dwelling place yet, had no need of a female servant, but Master Paget said at once that he was going to be wed and that he was certain his bride would require a personal maid."

Dear Lettice, with her pleasant face and her devoted ways, who never grew tired of singing the praises of the two young gentlemen! Well, at least she would be pleased by any alteration in the house!

Abigail, busy with her own thoughts, had mounted and was heading Cora down the bridle path that led through the small wood. The pony knew the way to her former master's home well and needed no guidance, but on this occasion she shied away from the path, whinnying.

"What's wrong, girl? What ails you?' Abigail tugged at the reign, speaking soothingly. Cora was gentle but, when complete strangers were about, she occasionally grew nervous. John Bailey had mentioned this peculiarity to Abigail, but it was the first time she had witnessed it for herself.

She peered ahead into the green-shadowed tunnel of interlaced branches but could see nothing unusual. Then she heard what Cora had already sensed. There was the crack of a twig and the faint rustling of leaves as something, or someone, moved deeper into the undergrowth. It was probably a poacher, but the knowledge that she was being watched was an uncanny feeling and, after a brief hesitation, Abigail wheeled the pony around and took the longer road that skirted the trees and wound over the meadow.

She reached Delaney Court without mishap and went at once to find Lettice and expound her plans for the improvements she intended to make. As she had expected the maidservant was delighted.

"This may be a very grand house, mistress, but there's no real comfort here, if you know what I mean," she said. "I think that it needs light and colour to bring it to life."

"We'll begin on the hall," Abigail told her. "I've had word that Master Paget is returning in two weeks' time, but we ought to be able to make a start."

"It'll require a thorough scrubbing," Lettice warned. "Those walls are thick with candle-grease."

"Then we'll get everybody on the task first thing in the morning," Abigail said briskly.

The prospect of having something definite to do filled her with a kind of elation. The servants too, rather to her surprise, appeared willing to carry out her orders although it entailed a great deal of additional work for them, but she guessed that they regarded the improvements as a symbol of the change in ownership. She fancied, too, that a few of them looked at her more kindly as they began to think that she might be a nicer person than they had suspected.

From dawn to dusk the great hall and the parlour leading off it were cluttered with brooms and pails and cakes of beeswax. Abigail had ordered that the tapestries be stripped, and the wood beneath cleaned and polished, the chimneys swept and the hearths filled with apple logs. Two rusting suits of armour were replaced by tables on which stood copper bowls filled with armfuls of flowers. She had found some magnificent pieces of silver and, when they had been cleaned, they made a sparkling display on the long table.

"When the master returns we will eat supper here as it must have been in the old days," Abigail said.

They had always eaten their evening meal as a family at home, the servants taking their places below the salt, her father at the head of the table. She pictured this table, gleaming with silver, with Paget in the high-backed chair. He would look magnificent, with his long black hair waving to his broad shoulders, and his smile a whiteness in the dark planes of his face. A sudden longing for him swept over her, and she turned aside abruptly and went into the parlour.

This apartment too had been transformed. A crimson carpet was laid on the floor and curtains of a similar shade hung at the windows. There were more flowers here too, a silver vase filled with long-stemmed red roses, a wide bowl filled with water on which tiny lilies floated. And on one wall she had hung an oval mirror, its gilt frame carved into cherubs' faces and thin-tailed mice. It was a charming mirror which she had discovered at the back of a cupboard in one of the upper rooms. Without knowing why, Abigail was certain that this had been her mother's mirror. She could imagine Jessica as a young girl, gazing into it and trying to picture what kind of a man she would eventually marry. Perhaps she had hoped that a knight on a white charger would ride into her life. Instead Josiah Lane had come, and Abigail suspected that not for a moment had Jessica ever seen him as the knight of her dreams.

Her own face gazed back at her out of the glass. Her daily rides had deepened the colour in her cheeks and her eyes were brilliant, as if her own longing were shining through them. There was a smear of dust on her cheek, and tendrils of brown hair had escaped from their severe coils to curl about her temples.

"I look like a kitchen wench," she said aloud, and laughed suddenly, pulling the remaining pins from her hair and letting it tumble down her back. Her slender frame was vibrant with an energy that flowed through her in wave after wave of tingling joy, a joy for which there was no reason save that she was young and her husband was coming home.

There were sounds of hoofbeats and the jangling of harness outside. Abigail's hands dropped to her sides and she swung about from the glass, joy bubbling into certainty. Paget was come home earlier than they had expected, and the only thought in her mind at that moment was that she must run to greet him, run to see the pleasure on his face when he walked into the gleaming, flower-decked hall.

He had already dismounted and was on the threshold of the open door when she skidded to a halt before him. His eyebrows rose in faint surprise as he straightened up from his bow, but his voice was as cool as ice-water sprinkled over her warm skin.

"I fear I arrive at an inconvenient moment, my love, I

wasn't aware you were in the midst of spring sweetening."

"You sent me no word." Her own voice was suddenly as flat and cold as his.

"John knew I was returning. He surely acquainted you with the fact."

"Yes." Abigail answered vaguely, her eyes flying to the young woman who had just entered and stood slightly in the rear. A tall Junoesque figure, with eyes as vividly blue as her travelling dress, the newcomer gazed about her, pushing back her hood to reveal hair as fine and bright as spun gold.

"Abigail, my dear, this is Henrietta Brown," Paget said, drawing the young woman forward.

Henrietta sank into a graceful curtsy, blue skirts billowing about her. "I am most happy to meet you, Mistress Abigail," she said.

Her clear, light voice was faintly accented. "Henrietta has lived on the Continent since she was a child," Paget said. "She is newly returned to England and in need of a position, so she will take over the duties of housekeeper."

"I shall take pleasure in the ordering of so fine a house," Henrietta assured them.

"Housekeeper? But we don't need—" Abigail had begun to stammer.

Henrietta Brown's amused blue glance swept over her. "But it is not fitting," she observed, "for the mistress to soil her hands when there are servants. I do assure you that such a thing shall not be allowed to occur again when I have begun my duties."

"First you must rest after the journey. Time enough for you to take up your duties tomorrow," Paget told her.

"Is there perhaps a room?" she enquired.

"About forty of them," Abigail said dryly.

"If you will come upstairs you may choose a room that pleases you." Paget had begun to guide her towards the stairs. Over his shoulder he said casually, "The hall is much improved, my dear. Pray compliment Lettice on her good taste."

CHAPTER SEVEN

LATER that evening Abigail sat at the long table, with anger rising up in her, as Paget and Henrietta chatted together about people and places they had known in France.

The newcomer sat opposite to her on Paget's left. Across the candlelit table her rosy face and bright blue eyes sparkled with animation and Paget inclined almost constantly in her direction, his eyes on her creamy shoulders which rose out of the pale gown she had chosen to wear. It was a gown more suitable for a ball than a family supper, Abigail thought, except that no decent woman would expose herself in such a manner even at a ball!

"And when the King made everybody believe that he was going to be married and even collected wedding presents from the French nobility!"

"Which he immediately pawned in order to pay his rent," Paget finished, and burst out laughing.

"That doesn't sound very honourable to me," Abigail said.

Paget gave Henrietta another smiling glance. "My lady wife is of the Puritan persuasion," he said. "That sect is noted for its lack of humour."

"As the Royalist party is noted for its coarseness," Abigail said sharply.

"Ah, mistress, we had little enough to amuse us,"

Henrietta said earnestly. "For many years we heard nothing but grim news of battles and saw nobody but those who had fled from the Roundheads. All seemed lost when King Charles was martyred, and for so long after that did we live in hope, praying for the restoration of the monarchy. You must not blame us if we laughed at foolish things, for there were often times when we wished to cry."

"The tears are over now," Paget said consolingly.

"And it does no good to dwell on the past," Abigail said, beginning to rise. "We have not yet discussed your duties if you're to be housekeeper, so perhaps you'd come into the parlour where we can talk."

"My wife means without any coarse Royalists to lower the tone of the conversation," Paget grinned.

"I will come at once, mistress," Henrietta said.

In the parlour Abigail took a chair and motioned the other to sit opposite. Wryly she thought they must present a complete contrast, she in her black dress with the white collar and Henrietta Brown in cream and pink lace.

"Your dress is not suitable for the occupation of housekeeper," she began.

"I have very few clothes," Henrietta said. "We tried to keep up appearances when we were in France, for it is easier to obtain credit if one is well dressed."

"Surely you have something more modest," Abigail asked.

"Yes, mistress, I have a very modest blue dress," Henrietta said demurely.

"How long were you in France?" Abigail asked curiously.

"My mother and I went out for a holiday when I was seven years old. Her mother was a Frenchwoman and lived in Paris. While we were there the war began, so we didn't come home. When I was nine we had word that my father had been killed and our home sequestered by the Roundheads, so after that we lived as we could. My mother died five years ago, and then my grandmother. She left me a little money but that's gone now, so I have to earn a living."

Despite herself Abigail couldn't help feeling a thrill of sympathy for the girl who had lost so much, and yet gallantly kept up appearances in a comely dress.

"You were going to tell me about my duties," Henrietta said.

"Duties, yes." Abigail bit her lip and tried to collect her thoughts. "You will be in charge of the other servants, except for my personal maid, Lettice. I shall require you to bring the supper menus to me every morning and a list of supplies to be ordered every month."

"Yes, mistress."

"As you saw tonight, there will be prayers at eight o'clock before supper every day, and I shall expect the servants to attend church whenever they possibly can. I believe there is a church four or five miles off."

"Have you not attended service there yet, mistress?" Henrietta asked.

Her face was the picture of innocence but Abigail frowned, aware of a pricking of guilt. "I've been very busy," she said, and despised herself for making excuses to the housekeeper.

"Yes, mistress?" Henrietta looked politely attentive.

"I intend to lighten up the entire house room by room," Abigail continued. "We will make plans for redecoration, but you will naturally defer to my wishes."

"Naturally." There was no mistaking the suppressed amusement in the other's voice now.

Choosing to ignore it, Abigail rose with what she hoped was quiet dignity, saying, "I trust you're comfortable in your room."

"Yes, mistress. I have a large apartment in the west wing and Paget said I could use the room next to it as a sitting room."

"Paget?"

"I beg your pardon!" A slender hand went up to the rosy lips. "We are old friends, so I am accustomed to use his Christian name. I must try to remember, mustn't I, that I am now only a servant!"

"Thank you. That's all." Abigail gave the other a brief, indignant nod.

Henrietta dipped into her irritatingly graceful curtsy and went out, closing the door softly behind her. Abigail stood irresolute for a moment. Paget would still be at table, toying with his wine goblet or peeling fruit with the tiny silver knife she had polished herself. It was the most natural thing in the world for a wife to join her husband, but she could not bring herself to open the door and walk out into the flower-decked hall, mellow now with the radiance of many candles. He had treated her with remote friendliness since his arrival, devoting his time to the new housekeeper in a way that must have seemed obvious even to the servants. Abigail was certain that by now they would be giggling in the kitchen over her discomfiture. She had almost donned the yellow dress, but to have done that would have been to admit that she was trying to attract him, and her pride would not allow that.

It was stupid to stand here alone. Impatient with herself, she opened the door and went into the hall.

Paget was not at the table. His half-empty goblet had been pushed aside, and only one small maid was clearing the dishes.

Abigail went slowly up the staircase and along the railed gallery. At the door of her room she hesitated and then went past towards the west wing. Candles had been lit along the passage and more light streamed from the open door a few paces ahead.

"My darling, if you could have seen how solemnly she said to me, 'Your gown is not suitable for the occupation of housekeeper'. She is very prim and proper, that one."

Henrietta's clear voice floated towards her on gurgles of laughter. There was an answering murmur, then Abigail picked up her skirts and ran back to the main wing and into her own apartment.

The fire and the candles had been lit, and Lettice sat waiting for her. "Is everything all right, mistress?" She rose, concern on her face, as Abigail slammed the door and stood, breast heaving, with her back against it.

"That female who came here today – do you know her?" Abigail asked tightly.

"Mistress Brown?" For an instant Lettice's voice wavered slightly. Then she shook her head, saying, "No, mistress, I was never in France, so how could I know her?"

"She behaves as if she were a guest, instead of the housekeeper," Abigail said.

"She's likely not used to being in service," Lettice said. "You must be patient with her, mistress, Master Paget was telling me what a hard time she'd had."

"Yes." Abigail moved to the fire and crouched by it,

warming her hands. As casually as possible she said, "I'm apt to forget they were friends before the restoration of the King."

"I believe that all the exiles sought one another's company."

"Yes, that's true, I suppose." Abigail dropped her gaze to the flames, seeing in them bright figures gallantly dancing in an alien land. Clearly Paget and Henrietta Brown had many experiences in common to remember, and this in itself would form a bond between them.

"Do you wish me to help you to bed, mistress?" Lettice was asking.

"No, I won't need you again tonight." The girl spoke absently, her gaze still on the dancing flames.

"Goodnight then, mistress." Lettice paused an instant as if she were going to say something else, but instead went quietly out.

My darling. That was what Henrietta Brown had said to Paget. *My darling darling darling darl—*. Abigail clapped her hands over her ears to shut out the mocking echoes, but they went on ringing inside her head in that cool, laughing voice with its intriguing hint of French accent. Paget had brought her to Delaney Court, believing that Abigail would be naive enough not to realise the truth they both flaunted. The tears she had held back for weeks flowed freely now, runnelling her cheeks, wetting the backs of her hands. She had never been more angry or more miserable, not even when Paget had first told her parents that he intended to marry her without dowry.

The next morning she woke heavy-eyed and listless, with fragments of disturbing dreams still clouding the edges of her mind. It was no comfort to have Lettice inform her that Master Paget had eaten already and ridden over to discuss estate matters with Master Bailey. "And Henrietta, Mistress Henrietta, is downstairs discussing tonight's supper menu with cook."

"Mistress Henrietta?" Reaching for her robe, Abigail lifted questioning brows.

"It is customary to employ the term when referring to a housekeeper," Lettice said, a tinge of reproach in her voice.

"Yes, of course." Abigail nodded and went over to the cupboards where her few dresses hung. Paget was out and would not have noticed even if he had been at home, but she added a pink scarf to her brown riding habit and tied back her hair with a matching ribbon.

Henrietta was in the hall when Abigail came downstairs, and one glance at her was sufficient to make the girl's heart sink. The housekeeper had put on the blue dress she had described as 'modest' the previous night. Certainly it was high in the neck and long in the sleeves, but its colour was a deep, shining blue figured with tiny blossoms of paler blue. She had coiled her golden hair into a coronet and tied a wispy lace apron about her waist. Her manner was so respectful that Abigail was certain that she had been practising it.

"If you please, Mistress Abigail, I have written the menu for your approval. Cook says there are trout if you would like a fish course, and she can make a cherry syllabub."

"That will do very well." Abigail glanced down the list without taking in any of the items properly and handed it back.

"Pag – Master Paget has gone to see his steward and won't be back until this evening."

"Yes, I know." Abigail cut her short.

"What orders do you have for me, mistress?" Henrietta asked.

"You may make your own rooms pleasant," Abigail decided, as cordial as it was possible for her to be over the anger inside her. "I told you this house was gloomy, so use what you need from the other rooms."

"That's very kind of you, mistress," Henrietta said meekly. "May I take blooms from the garden?"

"Yes. Yes, of course."

"Did you sleep well, mistress?" The pretty voice was gently enquiring.

"Not very well. I shall go for a ride and clear my head." Abigail walked past her to the main door.

Ten minutes later, mounted on Cora, she rode towards the woods. She had carefully chosen the opposite direction from the one in which John Bailey's house lay lest Paget catch sight of her, and jump to the conclusion she was seeking him. After what she had heard last night it was clear that he did not desire her company and was quite ready to join with Henrietta in mocking her.

It was a beautiful morning, rich and mellow as August should be before it slides into September. It was her duty to write to her parents and give them news of herself before the autumn rains made travelling more difficult, but when she thought of her father a dull resentment burned in her. For the sake of money he had forced her into a loveless marriage with a man whose motives were certainly suspect.

Cora jerked her head back, planting her forelegs so rigidly in the ground that Abigail was nearly thrown. They were in a dense part of the wood, and for an instant the girl fancied some animal must have startled the horse. Then she heard, as she had heard on the previous occasion, the snapping of a twig. Someone was definitely following her. She had the uneasy sensation of being watched, and for a moment her scalp prickled with fear. There were beggars and rogues everywhere, and though this was private land she had perhaps been unwise to ride alone so far from the main house.

"Who is it?" She wheeled Cora about and raised her voice. "Come out at once!"

"Abigail?" Thomas Wellborn emerged from the undergrowth and approached her.

"Thomas!" She dismounted and ran to meet him, surprise swallowed up in joy. "Was it you following me? Was it?"

"The other day too. I am lodging in Windsor and rode over."

"For what purpose? And why did you not call at the house?" she demanded.

"I might have done, but it was said in the village that Master Delaney had returned to Court. It would not have been seemly to have called upon you when your husband was away."

"Neither was it seemly to follow me!" she said sharply.

"I have been anxious," he said, "and that must be my excuse."

"Anxious about me?"

"There is nobody else in whom I have an interest, nobody else for whom I have an affection."

"But I am Paget Delaney's wife now," she said stiffly.

"Do you think that I had forgotten?" His voice was sombre. "I have thought of nothing else since I first learned of the offer that Master Delaney made."

"It was not an offer," she said. "The marriage was forced upon me."

"Forced upon all of us," he corrected. "I have realised ever since the wedding that I made the most terrible mistake in allowing myself to be threatened. You were right, Abigail, when you said that we could make a new life for ourselves in another land."

"It's too late." She had begun to tremble. "I am wed now and there's no going back."

"I had to see you again. I had to find out if you were well. I dare not hope you are happy; indeed, I am selfish enough to wish that you have not become reconciled to the situation."

"I have no choice but to be reconciled," she said. "I am Mistress Delaney now, and this is my home."

"And Paget Delaney is your husband." He reached out and took her hand, holding it between both his own, and fixed his mournful blue gaze upon her. "The knowledge has tormented me. Is he kind to you? He left you alone here for weeks, I understand."

"He was required at Court," she said.

"Aye, to fawn upon the Stuart."

"I was presented to the King," she said awkwardly. "He was very kind."

"He has filled the Court with loose women."

"Mistress Palmer," she nodded, "I saw her too."

"To take his bride into such company! I fear for you," he said gravely, "because he has begun to corrupt you. You calmly mention things you would not even have known about a few weeks ago."

"I have to grow up," she protested, withdrawing her hand.

"But not to lose your innocence!"

"Have you come here to scold me, Thomas?" she

said lightly. "You are not my betrothed now, you know."

"I only know that I am in the very depths of misery," he said. "I only know that I have followed you in the vain hope of catching a glimpse, of saying a few words to you. I had to know if your affections had altered."

Taken aback, Abigail stared at him, at his cropped fair head and pale face and anxious blue eyes. He was just as he had always been, and the emptiness inside her was just as it had always been.

"I am wedded now," she said breathlessly. "You have no right, no right—"

"Forgive me, but I could not help myself." He spoke tonelessly, his shoulders drooping.

"Let us talk of other things," she said. "My parents? Are they well?"

"I visited them once, about three weeks since. Your lady mother misses you sorely, but hopes you are settled and happy. She does not know that I am here, of course."

"And my father?"

"Is well. His pension was paid, so he said. It seems that Paget Delaney keeps his word."

"Did you think that he would not?"

"I expect nothing of value from Royalists," he said gloomily.

"They are only people, like us!" she exclaimed.

"Not like us," he corrected. "They have different standards of conduct."

"But not necessarily worse," she muttered.

"You have changed," he said sadly. "We never quarrelled before."

"And we are not quarrelling now!" In swift contrition she turned to him. "I feel as I always did, but the case is different now. I owe my husband loyalty at least, and he has a right to his views, as you have to yours. But it's too late now to talk of what might have been, and you do wrong to try to see me."

"I am justly rebuked." His tone and face were so downcast that she said encouragingly,

"But I am glad to see you again for all that."

"And I to see you."

He would have taken her hand again, but she moved away saying, "No. No, we will bid each other farewell now, and not meet again unless it be in company."

"It would not be kind of you to expect me to meet you as if there were nothing between us," he said.

"Then we'll not meet at all," Abigail answered. "You have all my good wishes, Thomas. You know that."

"And affection?" His eyes pleaded with her. "Have I that, Abigail?"

"What I can give you without dishonour," she said in a low voice.

"There is something I want you to have." He reached into his jacket and brought out a small, slim package wrapped in dark paper and sealed.

"Give me your word you'll hide this away and not open it until Yuletide," he said.

"I cannot accept gifts," she began, but he pressed the packet into her hands, saying earnestly, "This is a token of my enduring affection. Keep it hid until Yuletide and then open it."

"Why must I wait until Yuletide?" she demanded.

"Because it is the season when old friends remember one another," he said gravely.

"Then I thank you." She put the gift inside her cloak. "I will open it at Yuletide."

"Dear Abigail." His voice was gentle as he leaned to kiss her hand.

"I have to go." She drew away, bowing her head briefly as she turned.

"You will remember me?" he said as she remounted.

"Yes. Yes, of course." She felt a sudden impatience with him, for there was an undercurrent of reproach in his voice as if she had been the one who had broken their plighted troth. He had no right to look at her in such a hangdog fashion, no right to seek a private meeting now that she was wed.

Without looking back, she flapped the reins over Cora's back and rode on through the woods towards the main road that curved back to the gates of Delaney Court.

It was almost time for luncheon. She rode into the stableyard, called to one of the lads to unsaddle Cora, and went on into the house. Two maids were chopping vegetables in the kitchen as she passed through, and she guessed, from the way in which they speeded up their work, that they had been talking about her.

She nodded briskly and went through the hall and up the staircase to her room. The hearth had been cleared and relaid in preparation for the chill of the evening, and the bed made.

Taking off her cloak, she held the sealed package in her hands and stared at it curiously. It was not heavy but it felt solid. For a moment the temptation to peep almost overcame her. But she had promised to hide it away until Yuletide, so after a little thought she tucked it beneath a pile of shifts in the bottom of one of the cupboards.

"If you please, mistress?" A tap on the door announced Henrietta.

The housekeeper had acquired a few speckles of dust on her lacy apron in the course of her labours, but she still looked distractingly pretty.

"What is it?" Abigail asked.

"There is a spinet in one of the upper rooms, mistress," Henrietta said, " 'tis still in reasonable tune. I wondered if I might have it taken to my room."

"Do you play?"

"Yes, mistress. I have always taken great pleasure in music."

"And in dancing too, I suppose?"

"Oh, yes!" Henrietta's bright eyes sparkled. "I used to love to dance."

"I never learned," Abigail said wistfully.

"Then I am not to use the spinet?"

"No, you may have it. Two of the men will carry it for you."

"Thank you, mistress." Henrietta dropped a curtsy and went out again.

"I must be a complete fool," Abigail thought dismally, "to put such a weapon into her hands. Now she will delight Paget with her playing, perhaps even dance for him. And I can do neither. Nothing I do pleases him."

The realisation depressed her all over again.

CHAPTER EIGHT

IT was as she had feared. Later that evening, after another supper filled with uncomfortable pauses, Abigail was on her way to her room when she heard from the west wing the tinkling notes of the spinet. She hesitated, caught by the gaiety of the tune, her foot gently beating out the rhythm, and then above the music rang out Paget's laughter. Her own impulse to gaiety died, and she went silently into her room. It was useless to have thought, if only for a moment, that she could have joined them and shared in their pleasure. As she was dropping off to sleep the picture of the two of them, perhaps sitting close together, flashed, cruelly brilliant, behind her closed eyelids.

It rained the next day, water splashing from the gutters, streaming down the windows. Overhead the sky was a leaden grey. Abigail ordered the fires to be lit and went into the parlour where Paget was hunched over the table with account books before him.

"Is Master Bailey coming today?" she asked.

"Not if he's sensible! This weather will give a man the ague as quickly as anything can."

"Do you suffer from the ague? I have a remedy."

"The only thing I suffer from is boredom," Paget said, yawning. "I've done nothing since I came from Court but go through business documents. John Bailey has every fact at his fingertips and doesn't realise that I have been away for years!"

"You have not told me how it was at Court, at the naval review," she ventured.

"I didn't know you were interested," he said. "It would not have been much to your taste, I fear. There was a great deal of merriment there."

"You talk as if I were against all pleasures," she said, flushing deeply. "Life ought to have some amusements when work is done."

"What do you suggest, my dear wife?" He leaned back in his chair, regarding her from half-closed eyes.

"It's too wet to ride," Abigail said.

"That's remarkably observant of you, my love! It is indeed too wet to ride. Shall we roll dice together?"

"I don't know how to – roll dice," she said.

"Cards then? I have a pack somewhere, or don't you know how to play cards either?"

"We never played such games," she said humbly.

"What did you do at home when the weather was bad?" he asked curiously.

"Why we—" Abigail stopped, trying to remember just what they had all done when it rained. "My mother used to read aloud," she said at last. "She read very prettily. My father often complimented her on it."

"Well, I can't seriously see myself listening with rapt attention to you reading aloud to me," he said.

"I don't read as prettily as my lady mother," Abigail said.

"I could teach you to play chess," he suggested.

"Yes. Yes, I'd like to learn that," she began eagerly, but was interrupted by a knock on the door.

"Come in, come in!" Paget's lean face brightened

and he rose, holding the door wider. "Don't stand in the doorway as if you were a servant."

"It's just the menu," Henrietta said. "Cook thought you might fancy a stuffed duckling with some carrots."

"Sounds fine. We'll have that." He tossed the menu on to the table and smiled at Henrietta. "What do you do when it rains?" he enquired.

"To amuse myself? Why, I dance and sing a little, play chess and cards," she said.

"Then, if you've nothing better to do, perhaps you'll have a game of chess?" Paget said.

"Yes, of course," she began, then glanced at Abigail questioningly.

"I won't need you again this morning," the girl said dully. Too proud to show her hurt, she bowed slightly and went into the hall.

She had decided to get a book from the two or three dozen volumes in the library and was on her way there when Lettice came in.

"I've been talking to some of the other servants," she said, "and they tell me that others in the district have been given permission to go to the Michaelmas Fair."

"What's that?" Abigail asked.

"A day of merrymaking," Lettice said, looking faintly surprised. "Before the war there used to be many such fairs with pretty things to buy, and jugglers, and music, and dancing. Did you never go to one, mistress, when you were a child?"

Abigail shook her head silently. Such frivolities had been classed as wicked in her father's eyes.

"The Fair used to be held in honour of St. Michael who drove Satan from heaven," Lettice volunteered, "so there's no harm in it, mistress."

"Then I see no harm in their going," Abigail

decided. "We have to move with the times a little, I suppose."

"It would do you good to go," Lettice said, in a little burst of frankness. "You're too solemn and serious for your years, mistress."

"And this house makes me more so!" Abigail said impatiently. "It's dark and gloomy, and I expect to bump into Uncle Henry Delaney every time I turn a corner. We'll spend the rest of the day planning those improvements we talked about. This room needs pale hangings and more comfortable chairs. More books, too. The bindings of these are thick with dust."

"The master's at home. Shouldn't you discuss it with him?"

"The master has other matters to attend. Anyway, I have something else, a surprise I want to plan."

"Yes, of course." Lettice's quiet face brightened.

"We must have neighbours," Abigail said, "but nobody has called upon us since we came here."

"Cook said—" Lettice stopped, biting her lip.

"Cook said what?"

"That as you are Puritan, mistress, people may be shy of calling, for 'tis known that Puritans keep themselves to themselves."

"But I like company as well as anybody," Abigail said indignantly.

"Yes, mistress, but other people don't know you."

"And never will, if they don't call." Abigail drew Lettice down to the sofa and spoke quickly and eagerly. "That's what I've been thinking about. I want to give a supper party for a few people. We can get the house ready by – is it a long time to Michaelmas?"

"About a month, mistress."

"Then we'll make a start," Abigail said briskly.

"The day before the fair we will have the neighbours to come for supper and music. We'll have dancing too. Can you dance, Lettice?"

"I used to know the old country measures," Lettice said, "but it's years since I danced."

"I want you to teach me," Abigail said. "We will keep the matter between ourselves, as a surprise for Master Paget."

"Yes, mistress."

"And I will have a new gown," Abigail decided. "There are rolls of material in the room upstairs where my aunt's things are stored. Can you make me a gown, Lettice, a really lovely dress? Can you?"

"I've always been handy with a needle," Lettice said.

"We'll go up now and have a look through them." Abigail rose, eager to be busy. If she kept busy she might be able to shut out of her mind the parlour where Henrietta and Paget amused themselves over a game of chess.

In the long apartment with the shrouded furniture the two of them unrolled silk, velvet and brocade with mounting excitement.

"All this must have been part of my aunt's dowry," Abigail marvelled. "She was probably so miserable that she never even bothered to have them made up into garments."

"The moth got into some of them," Lettice said, "but there's plenty left for a dozen gowns. What colour will you choose?"

"This is pretty." Abigail held up a length of white satin patterned with tiny red and gold roses.

"With an overdress of pale green silk," Lettice said, "and white gauze at the elbows and shoulders with knots of green ribbon. Clothes are becoming much more elaborate."

"Yes, and the lady of the house ought to be in the fashion," Abigail agreed.

For the rest of the day the two women were occupied in cutting and measuring, pausing only for a brief nuncheon of cheese and bread. The rain still streamed down but Paget and Henrietta, according to Robin who brought up the food, had gone out to the stables to check on a new foal. His tone of voice and his expression told her, as clearly as if he had spoken it aloud, that the entire situation amused him mightily.

John Bailey arrived before supper, rain dripping from the brim of his hat and the collar of his cape. Paget, greeting him as Abigail came downstairs, said in a jocular fashion, "You smelled the roast duckling and you could not resist it! But we are about to have prayers, so you will have to suffer for your supper."

"I grew quite accustomed to praying during the years I served your father," John Bailey said calmly. "Good evening, Mistress Abigail. You have made an immense improvement here, if I may say so."

"You're very kind, Master Bailey." She clasped hands warmly.

"You're also dripping all over the carpet," Paget pointed out. "Robin! Come and take Master Bailey's garments and see that they're dried. You haven't met my old friend, Henrietta Brown. She has just come from France and is acting as housekeeper for us."

"Mistress Brown." The steward bowed, his eyes on the housekeeper's blue gown.

"If you will excuse me, I'll go and tell cook there will be an extra place at table," Henrietta said.

"Did you come over to see the new foal?" Paget

enquired, drawing John Bailey towards the fire. "Henrietta has named it Beau, because she declares the little fellow is the handsomest animal on the estate."

"I brought the account for the carriage you've ordered, sir," the steward said. "You'll be buying horses too, I suppose?"

"A pair of matched greys," Paget nodded. "I hope to ride over to Newmarket in a week or two and see what I can pick up there."

"Will you be going, mistress?" John Bailey turned to her politely but Paget answered, his voice casual.

"My lady wife has her house to attend. As you noticed, she has already begun to improve it."

"And I shall be occupied with preparations for Michaelmas," Abigail put in.

"You intend to celebrate Michaelmas?" John Bailey asked in surprise.

"One must move with the times," Abigail said lightly. "I shall hold a small supper party on Michaelmas Eve. You will come, I hope."

"I shall be happy to come," he bowed. "On Michaelmas Eve?"

"So that the servants will be free on the day of the fair," she said sweetly. "It ought to be a most pleasant day. Shall we go to prayers now? If we delay too long the ducklings will be spoilt."

She had the satisfaction of watching the casual contempt on Paget's face turn to unwilling admiration as she went past him into the long, narrow room where prayers were held.

Paget, no doubt with the ducklings in mind, hurried through the service with barely decent haste and within a short space of time they were seated at the long table, with John Bailey in Henrietta's place.

For most of the meal the conversation was confined to estate matters. There were three cottages that needed repair; a woman in the village was claiming poor relief though it was known her husband had refused to work for months; there was to be a cattle sale at Windsor with rumours of good beasts going cheap; there was a glut of apples and it might be a good idea to sell them before the price fell too sharply.

"Cannot we give them away, in charity?" Abigail interposed.

"In charity? Is that what you would do?" Paget asked.

"It was the custom at home," she said in a low voice, the colour rising in her face.

"Then we'll give the surplus away," Paget said, and the look he gave her was kinder than any look he had bestowed on her since his return.

"I meant to tell you, sir," John Bailey said, "that we had a stranger in the village the other day."

"Oh?" Paget gnawed on a wing and glanced enquiringly at the steward.

"I didn't see him myself," John Bailey explained, "Harry Wainwright told me that the man had stopped him and enquired if you were at home."

"Did he give a name?"

"No, but he was in Puritan dress. Young with fair hair, Harry said."

"Young, with fair hair," Paget repeated thoughtfully. "Has anyone called during the time I've been away, Abigail?"

She had blushed fiercely, and now felt colour ebbing from her face as Paget looked at her.

"Nobody called," she said at last, dropping her eyes to her plate, and feeling exactly as she had felt years before when her father had accused her of stealing a pear. Although the ripe fruit had actually fallen at her feet from the tree, she had felt as guilty as if she had climbed up to wrest it from the branch.

To her relief John Bailey, as if aware of her embarrassment, said, "The few neighbours we have live at some little distance. Would it help you if I drew up a list and then you could approve it?"

"It would be a tremendous help," she said gratefully.

"We could ask the Mainwarings," Paget suggested. "Peter Mainwaring had many an escapade with me when we were lads together."

"There are the Griffins too, sir," John Bailey said.

"Lord! Are they still in the neighbourhood? I remember being forbidden to play with the children because they were Royalist."

"And still are, sir. They lost their money during the war, but they hung on to their land and worked it themselves."

"Then they'll be glad of a good supper! How many will we be, d'ye think?"

"Twenty is a good round number," Abigail suggested.

"Am I to attend this supper?" Henrietta enquired, a slightly plaintive note in her voice.

"You will be fully occupied in the supervision of the servants, I imagine," Abigail said, "but I've no objection to your joining the company for a while."

Henrietta looked mutinous but bowed her head silently. Abigail, glancing nervously at Paget, was surprised to see amusement in his eyes.

"Will you have music, mistress?" the steward asked.

"If musicians can be found."

"Oh, there'll be fiddles and viols hidden away ready to be tuned," Paget assured her.

"We could bring down the spinet." Abigail, anxious to show generosity now that she had scored a point, smiled across at the housekeeper. "Henrietta plays beautifully, and would delight the guests."

Again she caught a look of amusement on Paget's face, and then he was talking gravely to the steward about the harvest, speculating as to whether the rain had spoiled the crops.

John Bailey's arrival had made the evening more bearable. By the time he left, refusing the offer of a bed for the night because the rain had stopped, Abigail felt relaxed and almost happy.

She dismissed Lettice and took down the book she had chosen earlier that day. It was a volume of poems, and she wondered if her mother had ever sat here as a girl, reading them and wishing that a handsome young man would carry her away. And in the end she had married Josiah.

"Can you spare me a few moments?" The door had opened and closed quietly without her noticing, and Paget stood there.

"Yes. Yes, of course." She too spoke politely, but her heart had begun to thump a little.

"You are certain that nobody called while I was away?" Although his voice was casual he came directly to the point and his grey eyes were alert.

"I did say so," she returned.

"It merely struck me that you seemed a little discomposed when the subject was brought up," Paget observed. "I have no objection to your receiving visitors."

"I told you that nobody called," she said, her voice

rising slightly. "That's why I decided on the supper party, so that people would visit. You don't object, do you?"

"Not at all. I welcome the notion of holding open house. My father was not a man who enjoyed the company of his fellows."

"You are going to Newmarket to buy horses, you said?"

"I've ordered a carriage," he told her. "My father always refused to keep one, but I am not like my father."

"He sounds, from what I've heard, like a very unamiable man," she admitted.

"A Puritan of the old school," he said grimly.

"But we are not all like that!" she said earnestly. "There are good and gentle people among us. We are not all hard and unforgiving. My mother—"

"Is a sweet-tempered lady who ought to have met a better husband," he interrupted. "I have kindly memories of Aunt Jessica from my childhood. I hope she is well."

"Oh, yes, though she misses me." Abigail could have bitten off her tongue the next moment for Paget was staring at her.

"How do you know that?" he demanded.

"Why, a letter—" she began, caught at a loss.

"No letters have been delivered here, save my own to John Bailey telling him to expect my return."

"You cannot possibly be sure of that," she objected.

"But if your mother had written then you would have mentioned it to me," he returned, "so perhaps you would do me the favour of being honest and telling me exactly how you knew your mother is well but misses you."

Abigail had risen from her seat and taken a few agitated steps towards the window. She was aware of his eyes boring into her back, and though he had not raised his voice there was a steely quality in it that made her tremble.

"Very well, very well." She swung about, clenching her hands. "I didn't receive a letter from my mother. It was Thomas Wellborn who told me she was in good health."

"You said that nobody called."

"He didn't call. I met him purely by chance when I was out riding."

"Master Wellborn lives a journey of three days off, and you met him by *chance*!"

"He was lodging at Windsor and came to find out how I was. Hearing that you were away he did not wish to compromise my honour by coming to the house."

"He preferred to sneak about and meet you in the woods, I suppose."

"He was betrothed to me and has an interest in my welfare."

"I am wed to you and have an interest in your reputation."

"Which has not suffered, because nobody saw me. And you're a fine one to prate of reputation!" she flared. "You go away for weeks and don't even trouble to let me know when you're returning, and when you do come you bring that – that *housekeeper* with you."

"Are you jealous, my love?" His long fingers gripped her forearms and his eyes challenged her.

"Of Henrietta Brown?" She forced scorn into her voice, though her legs were trembling. "I care not a jot what you choose to do with your free time. It does not compromise me!"

"So you choose to compromise yourself without my help, is that it? You meet that canting lawyer who was ready to abandon you to save his precious licence."

"You threatened him!"

"And bribed your father. It was interesting to see how quickly they both threw you to the Royalist wolf! But then I was determined to marry you."

"Aye, to win your wager!" She twisted out of his grasp and faced him, panting. "And you will not win it, for we may be married but I'm not yet your wife!"

"I have a remedy for that," he said softly, and before she could protest, he had seized her in an embrace as punishing as it was passionate. One hand held her to him, the other gripped her long hair, forcing back her head as his lips crushed her own into helpless surrender. Shudders of desire racked her and a sweetness that was almost painful in its intensity welled up from the depths of her nature. Vaguely she was aware of a ripping sound as the thin silk of the robe she wore tore between his hands. His lips moved from her mouth to her neck and her back arched against him in an unendurable hunger for fulfilment.

"Wife," he said hoarsely, raising his head. "My wife!"

His eyes glowed with triumph, and opening her own eyes upon his boldly handsome face, Abigail was suddenly as still as stone. She had reminded him that she was not yet his wife, and he had accepted her challenge, glorying in her weakness.

She drew a deep breath, her voice coming out like drops of ice. "The wager was that you could make me love you. This is not the way."

"You want me. You know that you do!" he interrupted.

"Wanting is not loving. So you'd not win the wager."

"Damn the wager!" His face was savage now.

"And you'd not enjoy me," she said. "If you take me like this you'll not enjoy it."

For a moment she thought that he was not going to listen to her, and gladness leapt up in her, but even as she felt herself begin to weaken into his arms again he had loosed her and stepped back, the savagery in his face hardening into something more terrible, for it was gentle and remote as if he had gone a long way away, though in fact he had stepped back only a pace.

"You place a high value on yourself," he said. "One day, madam, you may find a man willing to pay the price."

She opened her mouth with no clear idea as to what she intended to say, but it made no matter for he gave her one long, sweeping glance that shrivelled her into nothingness, then turned on his heel and strode out.

The slam of the door echoed in her ears and then there was no sound but the crackling of the wood on the hearth. Abigail sank into her chair and pulled her torn robe more closely around herself. Surely if he had loved her, he would have stayed. Perhaps, if she had allowed him to make love to her, then he would have really loved her when it was over. The tragedy of it was that now she would never know.

She rose at last and went over to the window to pull back the curtains. The moon had risen and the garden below was bathed in silver, the yews standing like sentinels above the grass. As she looked down a figure moved out of the shadows into the moonlight and was silhouetted there. She drew back, peering through the rain-spotted pane, but the figure was so muffled in cloak and hat it was impossible to distinguish if it were man or woman. As she gazed a cloud crossed the moon and the figure was gone.

Abigail let the curtain fall back into place and went over to the fire again. As a small girl she had sometimes watched the fire die down and pictures form in the flames of ships and castles and fairies – though her father declared there were no such things. But tonight the only pictures that formed were in her own mind, pictures of herself in years to come sitting alone night after night, of Paget walking past her closed door towards the west wing where the spinet constantly played mockingly and gaily, of a cloaked figure watching the house in the moonlight.

She had meant to please her husband, to make him love her, and she had spoiled it all. Sadly she thought that there seemed to be two different people inside her. One was loving and passionate, the other was prim and unforgiving. And each of the girls inside her disapproved of the other.

CHAPTER NINE

DURING the days that followed Abigail devoted her time to the redecoration of the house, and seldom saw Paget, who rode away from Delaney Court early every morning and didn't return until supper time, when he acknowledged her coolly and then devoted himself to Henrietta. The two of them chatted almost without pause about the times they'd shared in France when there had been no money but a warm comradeship that had bound the Royalist exiles together.

Abigail listened silently, her face calm above the white collar of her black dress, anger rising in her at this open humiliation. Yet perhaps Paget had some reason to behave as he did, for having agreed to marry him she was, in duty, obliged to submit to him, and this she had refused to do. The law permitted men to rape and beat their wives, and nobody at all considered it was necessary to marry for love.

'He may not love me, but he is beginning to respect me,' she thought, but the knowledge gave her scant comfort during the hours after supper when she sat alone in the luxury of her room, knowing that Paget was in Henrietta Brown's sitting room.

Abigail had to admit that the young woman made herself useful. She was indefatigable in rooting out pretty ornaments and lacy covers from the backs of cupboards where they had remained for years, and her ideas for brightening the house were lively and accorded with Abigail's own.

"Light and space and gaiety are fashionable now," she declared. "People are getting rid of these dusty tapestries and beginning to lay carpet instead of rushes on the floors."

"It will make the rooms much colder," Abigail objected, but she was pleased with the effect as room after room was transformed. The floors of stone and wood were polished and laid with bright carpets, pale drapes hung at the windows, dainty china and gleaming silver ornamented the tables, and loose drapes of velvet and brocade softened the outlines of heavy, dark furniture.

The great hall, parlour, library, and drawing room were finished. Abigail decided that she would start on the upper floors after Michaelmas, though she suspected that her uncle's apartments would resist her efforts. At least she had succeeded in banishing his influence from the reception rooms.

She and Lettice found time in which to practise the steps of the country dances the maidservant knew. At first Abigail felt awkward and foolish but, as Lettice hummed the airs, so a natural sense of rhythm came to the girl's aid and she began to move with more confidence.

"You're light on your feet, mistress," Lettice complimented.

"Light of foot, heavy of heart," Abigail said.

"Ah, well, matters will change," Lettice said with an air of knowing more than she would tell.

"Michaelmas should cheer us all," Abigail commented.

She had sent out invitations to a dozen families in the

district and received acceptances from all but two. She suspected that most of them were coming out of curiosity to see her and to take a peep at the big house where Henry Delaney had lived secluded, but the important thing was that they should come. Surely there would be a few among them who would like her and cultivate her friendship.

"There's a rider coming up the drive," Lettice announced. "I think he's a post boy."

Abigail hurried down to the hall. Paget had gone over to Newmarket to buy his horses, but it was unlikely that he would bother to write. As she reached the door she was in time to see Henrietta running to meet him. The housekeeper stood for a few moments talking to the rider who handed her two letters, then trotted round to the back, no doubt to claim refreshments in the kitchen.

"Henrietta!" Abigail raised her voice to call, and in a flash one of the letters was tucked into the other's pocket which hung from her waist like a reticule, and Henrietta turned slowly, the remaining missive in her hand.

"It's for you, mistress, from Oxfordshire," she said.

"And the other?" Abigail queried.

"Other, mistress?" The blue eyes were innocent.

"The one you put away," Abigail said.

"It was from – from an old friend of mine," Henrietta said. Her face had crimsoned, but there was an excited little smile playing about her lips.

"I see." Abigail held out a hand for her own letter. Every nerve in her wanted to shriek, 'Paget wrote to you, didn't he? Why don't you say that you're his mistress?'

But if she said that she would lose her last shred of dignity.

In the parlour she sat down to read the letter from home. It was in her father's handwriting and began, as she might have expected, with a complaint.

'My Dear Abigail,

'As you have been somewhat remiss in your duty and not written, I take pen in hand to assure you that your lady mother and I are well in health and trust that you have settled with resignation into the estate of matrimony.

'I trust also that you are dealing with the house-keeping in the way you have been trained and are not allowing your servants to idle or gossip. I am certain that it is not necessary to remind you that a period of quiet prayer once or twice a day is of inestimable value, and that now you are a wife, sobriety of dress and of conduct are most important. Indeed these may be the means by which you bring Master Delaney to a practice of virtue. A good wife may indeed be priced above rubies.

'Your lady mother and I join in wishing you well, and trust that you will not grow proud in the estate in which you find yourself.

Your loving father,

Josiah Lane.'

"Puritan cant!" Abigail exclaimed aloud and flung the letter down. She could just imagine her father sitting down to write it, a complacent look on his face. He might well look complacent with his pension doubled, his fine paid, and his daughter married off without dowry to a very rich man!

And he had given her no real news at all. He hadn't told her how the servants did, or if the cat had had any more kittens, or if her mother missed her. He had simply lectured her about duty and hoped she had not grown proud in her estate!

"My estate," Abigail muttered, "is no cause for pride, father dear. My husband first made it clear that he had married me for a wager, and now makes it even clearer that he has no intention of trying to win it!"

Angrily she scrunched up the letter and thrust it into the fire. The post boy was probably in the kitchen, waiting for a reply. She tightened her lips and went through to the hall, calling Lettice.

"Yes, mistress?" The maid, a pile of clean linen in her arms, was coming downstairs. "Were there letters?"

"For me and Mistress Henrietta. Mine was from my father."

"Not bad news, mistress?"

"No news at all," Abigail said briefly. "Go and find Henrietta and ask her to check the linen. That's her task, not yours."

"Yes, mistress." Lettice bobbed a curtsy and scurried off.

The linen room was at the top of the house and would keep Mistress Henrietta safely out of earshot.

Abigail waited a few minutes and then went casually through to the kitchen. As she had expected the post boy was there, surrounded by giggling servants as he partook of refreshments, but he rose as she came in, saying, "Will there be a reply, mistress?"

"No reply. What do I owe you for the letters?"

"Nothing. The other young lady paid." He pushed aside his mug and reached for his hat. "I hope 'twas a good letter, mistress."

"So dull that if I'd known the contents I'd have sent it back unpaid," she sad wryly.

"Postage is expensive," he agreed.

"And it's three days' ride to Oxfordshire and – how far in the other direction?" She began to walk with him through the back door where stone passages led past dairy and buttery to the stable yard.

"Oh, Newmarket is a way off," he said, "but I'm given the mail in London by the relay riders, so I only have the one journey to make. Good day to you, mistress."

So Paget had written to Henrietta as Abigail had suspected. She inclined her head in silence, and went back into the kitchen, her voice sharpening as she noticed the maids still lounging at the table.

"Have you no work to do?"

"Yes, mistress." One of the older girls hesitated, then said, "We were telling Phyllis here that there are no such things as ghosts."

"I never said it was a ghost," the girl called Phyllis argued. " 'Twas a solid man."

"Where?" Abigail asked.

"Outside the house, mistress, looking about the place. It seemed to me that he was waiting for someone."

"When was this?"

"Twice, mistress. I saw him a couple of weeks ago, and then again last night. I got up in the night and he was outside, standing at the side of the house, all muffled up in a cloak and hat so I couldn't see his face."

"Where is your room?" Abigail asked.

"We all sleep in the east wing," the third girl said.

"It was probably one of the menservants checking the locks."

"No, mistress, it was a stranger," Phyllis insisted. "I couldn't see his face, but I knew it was a stranger."

"We ought to have dogs here," one of the other girls said. "The old master didn't like animals in the house, but I'd feel safer with two or three big dogs to guard and give warning."

"I'll speak to Master Paget about it when he returns," Abigail promised.

She reflected uneasily on what Phyllis had said as she went out again. So the darkly muffled figure had been neither a figment of her imagination nor one of the estate workers. She had dismissed the incident from her mind, but now it seemed the figure had been seen the previous night too.

Perhaps Thomas Wellborn had come back in order to try to see her again. It was flattering to think that perhaps he still held her in such affection that he could not keep away, but it was also dangerous, because Paget had already shown himself to be jealous. It was a pity that his jealousy sprang, not from love, but from his desire to possess her.

Abigail decided that it would be wise to ride down to the village and make a few enquiries. If Thomas were still in the neighbourhood she would take the risk of trying to contact him and begging him to leave. After all, if Paget believed she was still seeing her former betrothed, then he might very well consider himself justified in keeping up his relationship with Henrietta.

The village was, as usual, almost deserted. Most of the men were bringing in the harvest, and many of them had been joined by their wives. She had passed several women, skirts tucked up and kerchiefs on their heads, toiling in the fields and felt a wistful envy of them, because they looked content with their lot and not racked with hopes and doubts and conflicting emotions.

John Bailey had said that Harry Wainwright had mentioned a stranger having been in the district. Old Harry was retired now and spent most of his time either strolling about the place offering unwanted advice or smoking a clay pipe outside the small cottage where he lived with his son and daughter-in-law.

He was there when she rode up, a mug of ale at his elbow, blue smoke curling about his head. As Abigail dismounted, he took the pipe out of his mouth and greeted her with, "Good day, mistress. I'm sorry I cannot rise, but my rheumatics is mortal bad this afternoon."

'Which means he is hoping nobody will ask him to lend a hand with the reaping,' Abigail thought.

Aloud she said, "I'm sorry to hear that. You must try an infusion of elm bark. I'm told it's an excellent remedy."

"I fear I'm too old for anything to work," old Harry said mournfully. "I'm near eighty, you know."

"I thought you were seventy-three," Abigail said.

"Ah, well, I'm nearer to eighty than when I was twenty," he declared, slapping the table in delight at his own jest.

"That's very true," she agreed. "Not that you look your age. I'd have taken you for nearer fifty."

"I've got all my own teeth," he boasted, "which is more than my son can say! Mind, I need spectacles now, but my hearing's sharp, and I've all my wits about me."

"And you probably know everybody in the village," she said.

"Everybody, living and dead. Living *and* dead!" he repeated.

"You knew my uncle?"

"Worked for him nigh on sixty years," the old man said. "He was a hard man, was Master Delaney. Hard as nails but fair-minded. Very fair. He never turned a man off for sickness or old age. And he never held a man's private opinions against him neither, provided he kept them to himself."

"I take it you held different views," Abigail said, noting the long straggling white hair that had obviously never been clipped short.

"That I did!" old Harry said vigorously. "I was for King Charles, and if I'd been younger I'd have fought for him too. But I kept my mouth shut and did my work, and Master Delaney respected that. Not that I wasn't delighted when the King was restored, the new King. I'd have danced a jig, if my legs would have stood up to it. Aye, it's grand to see the old days coming back!"

"And there's the fair," Abigail reminded him.

"They tell me you have given the house servants leave to go."

"I am not against a little amusement," she said, "even if I am a Puritan."

"Ah, mistress, you're not like a regular Roundhead!" old Harry exclaimed. "You're like your lady mother used to be. She was gay and laughing, when the master wasn't looking."

"But everyone is a Royalist now, I suppose," she smiled.

"Not everyone. There are still some who ride around with long faces and plain suits," he returned.

"Master Bailey said you'd seen a stranger." Abigail saw her opportunity and took it.

"Asking questions about the master, if he was at

home and when he was expected back and so on. I gave him short shrift, I can tell you, mistress!"

"Have you seen him recently?" she asked.

"The master was over a day or two since, mistress."

"Not the master, I mean the stranger. The Puritan?"

"Asking questions. Whether the master is home."

"Have you seen him since then? Is he still in the neighbourhood?"

"Fair-haired, cropped short, without even a periwig. That was the one?"

Abigail nodded, trying to restrain her impatience.

"I only saw him the once," old Harry said. "I don't hold with Roundheads. Was there anything else you wanted?"

"No. I was just – curious, that's all. Master Paget doesn't like the idea of strangers on the estate, especially when he is away."

"Well, I sent him on his way," the old man said gleefully.

"And you've not seen any other strangers?" He shook his head. "Then I'll bid you good day." She smiled and remounted Cora, aware that he was staring at her inquisitively, the pipe still in his hand. No doubt he wondered why she was so interested in the stranger.

She waved her hand and rode on. So the man who had watched the house on at least two occasions might not have been Thomas Wellborn at all, unless he was lying low somewhere, and she considered that unlikely.

She decided that it might be wise to tell Paget about the man, and ask him to buy a couple of guard dogs so that the household might be more secure.

As she reached the stable yard Paget himself came striding out. "I come home to discover my wife is out," he began.

"If I'd known you were coming back today, I'd probably have stayed in," she said, "but as you never write to me, I cannot possibly be expected to sit tamely indoors waiting for you to decide to come home!"

"You must be the most ill-tempered woman I've ever met," he said, leaning against the stable door and making no effort to help her dismount. "Do cease your nagging for five minutes, and come in here. I want to show you something."

Abigail hesitated, then went through the door into the stable, and thence to the barn beyond. It was usually empty, but now a small carriage stood in the middle of it.

"Oak panelled and padded with silk and velvet," Paget said, "and I've bought four matched greys to pull it. What do you think?"

"It's fit for a King," Abigail breathed.

"Or a queen!" He opened the door and pulled down two steps. "Sit inside and then tell me if it isn't the best carriage you ever rode in!"

She climbed up into the vehicle and sat down cautiously.

"Well?" There was a boyish eagerness in his face.

"I never rode in a carriage before, but I cannot imagine a finer one," Abigail said. "Where are the new horses?"

"They're bringing them over in a day or two," Paget said. "I tell you, my love, we'll be the envy of the neighbourhood! What have you been doing with yourself while I was at Newmarket?"

"Getting ready for the Michaelmas party," she said. "You will be at home for it?"

"You think I might take it into my head to go away and leave you to face all the neighbours by yourself?"

"I never know what you'll take it into your head to do," Abigail said wryly.

"Rest assured that on the evening of the party I will be the devoted husband," he said, his eyes dancing.

"There'll be no need to overdo it," she said sharply.

"I'm entirely in your hands," Paget returned blandly. "Are we to have prayers before supper on that night?"

"No, of course not!" she began crossly, then laughed despite herself as she realised he was teasing her.

"You look so pretty when you laugh," he commented, "that I wish you would do so more often."

"I wish—" she began.

"What do you wish?" His face was gentler than she had ever seen it. She hesitated, wanting to tell him how she wished that the foolish wager had never been made, how she wished that he had never brought Henrietta to Delaney Court, how she wished that he would love her just a little before he tried to claim his marital rights.

There was the swift pattering of feet through the stables into the high barn and Henrietta's voice rang out. "Oh, Pag – Master Paget, is this the new carriage? Why, it's beautiful! Robin said that you had returned! You must be tired after so long a journey."

"I'll be in now, Henrietta." Paget had turned, his voice seemed to acknowledge the other's right to come in search of him.

"It is a beautiful carriage, is it not?" Abigail raised her own voice slightly as she began to descend.

"Mistress Abigail, I didn't see you there," Henrietta had stopped short, her face and voice becoming chillier.

"I was trying out the comfort of the seats," Abigail said. "Did you want something?"

"She rushed out to welcome me, didn't you, Henrietta?" Paget said. "And to offer me refreshment, I understand?"

"After your journey," Henrietta said, her blue eyes modestly downcast.

"Ah, you know how to look after a man!" Paget exclaimed. "I'm starving, if truth be told."

"There are fresh girdle cakes," Henrietta said as coyly as if she had made them herself.

"Then lead me to them!" Paget tucked her arm through his as they walked back into the stable.

Abigail stood by the new carriage, biting her lips in frustration. At the very moment when she and Paget stood on the verge of an affection that might grow into something richer and deeper, Henrietta came to spoil it all, and Abigail was left alone again. She stared gloomily at the coach, trying to recapture the feeling of pleasure that had bubbled up in her when Paget had first shown it to her, but she could only think of the way he had smiled when Henrietta came in. He had not even glanced back as he walked out.

She gave the shiny vehicle a last, disappointed look and trailed back through the stables, too dispirited even to stop and pet the new foal. After all, Henrietta had been the one who had named it Beau.

Paget was in the kitchen, a hot cake in one hand, his booted leg propped on a stool. Henrietta was standing by him, her voice sweetly persuasive. "It would be such a reassurance for the maids to have a dog, if Mistress Abigail has no objections."

"Why should I have any objections?" Abigail interrupted. She had meant her tone to be lightly teasing, but it merely sounded petty and carping.

"What's this about strangers around?" Paget demanded. "Have you seen anyone?"

"No." It was a foolish lie, but it came without thought, and she flushed miserably the moment the word was out, aware of the shrewd glance that Paget gave her.

"But you'd not mind a dog?" he said.

"I like dogs," she said. "I like dogs very much, and I think it would be a good idea to have one. I think it would be an excellent idea."

"Then we'll get one," he said, raising his eyebrows in faint surprise at the vehemence of her tone.

"And I will make certain that it doesn't disturb you," Henrietta said.

Always Henrietta, to say the wrong thing at the wrong moment! Abigail wanted to scream at them both, but the cook was listening and one of the maids had just come in. She inclined her head slowly, and went through to the hall, anger as strong as love inside her.

CHAPTER TEN

THE eve of Michaelmas was one of those golden days that gladden the heart and make one forget the approach of winter. In the morning the faintest touch of frost sharpened the beauty of leaf and flower, and the scent of burning apple logs pervaded the house. The servants were up before dawn preparing for the supper. It would be a lavish one of roast duckling and chicken, trout baked in cream sauce and sprinkled with almonds, cabbages stuffed with raisins, potatoes boiled in mint, a beefsteak pie, oyster patties, iced cakes thick with honey, frosted grapes, tarts filled with plums and quinces, lemon syllabub, strawberry jelly, and three kinds of cheeses. Those who were not occupied in cooking were decorating the rooms with great armfuls of golden rod and the long table gleamed with silver and crystal.

The main rooms looked very different from the gloomy caverns into which Abigail had walked three months before. With the dismal tapestries removed, the wood polished to shining perfection, mirrors reflecting the flowers and ornaments, Delaney Court was a beautiful and welcoming house. It was a pity that its outer aspect did not contain an inner harmony. Paget had not come to Abigail's room since the night she had repulsed him, and though his manner towards her was impeccable there was a coolness in it that cast down her spirits. He seemed to be on terms of the closest friendship with Henrietta but whether their relationship went beyond friendship was something that Abigail tried not to think about. During the day she was able to keep her mind occupied, but when darkness had fallen and Lettice had withdrawn, it was hard to banish the suspicion that Paget was in the west wing with the blue-eyed young woman whose plump white shoulders and sweet smile must surely attract any man.

Abigail's own mood became much more cheerful when she was dressed for the party and gazed at herself in the long pier glass. Lettice had done a wonderful job on the material they had found. The dress of pale green was open in front to show the petticoat of white satin with its pattern of tiny red roses. White gauze edged the puffed sleeves and the low neckline, and narrow green ribbon was knotted at the dipped waist. She had drawn her heavy brown hair back into a loose knot at the back of her neck, and her only jewellery were her wedding and betrothal rings. The emerald in its elaborate setting suited this fashionable gown better than her plain Puritan dress. Her eyes, long-lashed above delicate cheekbones, sparkled with pleasure at her own appearance.

"You look charming, my dear," Paget said from the doorway.

For an instant her breath caught in her throat as she turned to face him. He wore court dress of brown and gold with sash and breeches of pale green. The lace cravat that foamed over the satin waistcoat emphasised the lean, dark planes of his face with its jutting nose and firm mouth. His grey eyes surveyed her lazily. For a moment something glowed at the back of them, then the veil of cool friendliness dropped again and he said, "We ought to go down and greet our guests together. It's always advisable to keep up appearances."

"Yes, of course, but best not overdo it," she advised, "lest you startle the servants."

"Oh, I imagine they will be able to contain their feelings," he returned. "You are not wearing your necklace."

"Ostentation can so quickly become vulgarity," Abigail countered, ignoring his proffered arm and sweeping ahead of him into the corridor.

In the gallery the hired musicians were already tuning their instruments. Wreaths of ivy had been twined round the curved balustrade of the staircase and the rattle of harness announced the arrival of the first guests. For a moment Abigail's knees shook with nervousness. Then Paget's hand gripped her elbow and she was descending the staircase, her head high and a smile on her lips.

"Mistress Abigail, you look lovely." John Bailey emerged from a sea of faces and clasped her hands warmly.

"You're very kind," she said, allowing him to draw her aside. "This is a little confusing for me. All these people."

"Come out of curiosity and staying to admire," he said.

"Because I am Puritan. Do they think Puritans have two heads?" she asked a little indignantly.

"They wonder why Paget Delaney should return from exile and immediately marry one," he told her. "Now that they have seen you they will no longer wonder."

"You flatter me," she said.

"You forget that I am of the same persuasion as yourself," he corrected. "I never flatter married ladies, even when they are as pretty as you are."

"Mistress Abigail, shall we take our places at table now?" Henrietta was asking. "Cook is complaining that the syllabub will spoil if we wait longer."

"Very well." Abigail nodded, some of the gaiety draining out of her as she saw that the housekeeper had chosen a dress striped in ivory and gold. It was a simple gown, but it clung to her generous figure and it blended with Paget's suit in a way her own dress did not. Already she had heard Henrietta say "Gracious, no! I'm only the housekeeper!", in answer to some remark or other.

"I'll sound the gong," Henrietta said, bobbing a demure curtsy.

The gong echoed hollowly and the guests began to drift towards the table. Up in the gallery the musicians began to play softly. The candles had been lit and their glow cast a gentle radiance over the faces of the ladies and their gowns of silk and satin. Some of the dresses were not in the latest fashion, one or two of the velvet coats showed signs of discreet darning, and jewels were sparse. Abigail pictured the neighbours rummaging in the bottom of chests and at the back of cupboards for the finery they had not been able to wear before the King's restoration. More and more she was beginning to realise that there was a certain gallantry in the way they had clung to their hopes through eleven years of what they must have regarded as tyranny.

"So Paget has taken himself a wife, and a pretty one too!" declared a gentleman on her right.

"Thank you, sir." She turned to smile into a florid, elderly face.

"Mark Griffin, mistress." He indicated himself. "We were introduced earlier, but I doubt if you took in my name with so many strange people crowding upon you."

"It is a little confusing," she admitted. "We lived very quietly at home, and I am not accustomed to society."

"Neither have we been, these past years," he said wryly. "Life has been bleak. You know our son was killed at Edgehill?"

"No, I didn't know. I'm sorry."

"Paget has been kindness itself, helping in every way he can without making it seem like charity. You are fortunate to have such a kindly man, my dear, as he is fortunate in having chosen such a lovely wife as yourself."

Paget in the role of fairy godfather was an unfamiliar character to Abigail. She stole a glance at him from under her eyelashes, noting the hard line of his jaw, the long black hair that waved down his shoulders. Something inside her yearned for him to turn his head and smile at her.

"You come from near Oxford, do you not? The King held it for much of the war, but you are too young to remember that," Mark Griffin said to her.

"Yes. Yes, I was," she agreed.

"I saw his majesty once," he continued. "He was very small and thin, with a forked beard. The present King is a taller man, I understand?"

"Tall and black-haired," she nodded.

"Ah, something like Paget, then!" he began, but she cut him short impulsively.

"Paget is much better-looking than the King!" Her words fell into a little pool of silence. She blushed furiously, aware that every eye was fixed on her, that there were sympathetic smiles on many mouths.

"Your lady wife is not ashamed to reveal her admiration of you, Paget," another guest said. "I wish my own were as flattering!"

"You must not be embarrassed," Mark Griffin consoled. "It is a rare thing for a wife to love her husband these days."

Out of the corner of her eye Abigail could see the curl of Paget's lip, but his voice was pleasant.

"It is indeed unfashionable, but then Abigail and I don't care for current modes. We please ourselves, don't we, my sweet?"

"Yes, dear." She gave him a meek little smile, noting with satisfaction that his own eyes shifted to his plate and his mouth tightened. Paget Delaney was not accustomed to mockery, and this small triumph of hers evened the score between them.

The supper was delicious, the wines mellow. Abigail found that she was beginning to enjoy herself. Mark Griffin treated her with fatherly courtesy, and she found herself responding gaily. And all the time there was the yearning inside her towards the husband who smiled and chatted amiably, giving them all the impression that he was devoted to her, and playing the part so well that she was almost deceived herself.

The meal was drawing to its close, and her heart began to thud uncomfortably as she had remembered what she had planned. Nervously she rapped the goblet at her place with a spoon, and jumped slightly as the conversation died down.

"The drawing room has been cleared for dancing," she said loudly. "My husband I will lead the first set."

There were exclamations of pleasure mingled with

surprise. It was clear that though she had made a good impression they had not expected her to dance. Paget, his dark face impassive, rose and pulled back her chair, offering her his arm with an exaggerated politeness which those present evidently took for affectionate teasing, to judge by their genial laughter.

"Do you truly dance, or is this another attempt to make a fool of me in public?" he asked under cover of scraping chairs and rustling skirts.

" 'Tis a challenge," she answered.

"Then I accept it," he said promptly. "Mind, I'll make no excuses for you if you drag round like a sack of flour."

"Nor I for you if you tread on my toes," she retorted sweetly, and gasped as he swung her into the first circle of the measure.

Pacing out the steps with Lettice was quite a different matter from following the rhythm with other people hard on her heels and Paget's cynical gaze almost inviting her to make a mistake, but after a slightly faltering start Abigail began to enjoy herself. The music set her feet tapping and her body swaying, and Paget danced superbly, being light on his feet and gracefully certain in his movements.

"You're a creature of surprises," he murmured, holding her more closely as they paced. "Who taught you to dance?"

"Perhaps it was a handsome young man," she murmured provokingly, "or perhaps I learned it all by myself."

"What man? Thomas Wellborn?" His grip tightened on her hand.

"Him – or another!" She broke free, circling as the rhythm quickened.

"This is a kissing dance," Paget said as they linked arms again, "it ends with a kiss."

Lettice had not bothered to mention that. Abigail felt a thrill of what she chose to regard as distaste, but answered him lightly.

"You can pretend to sprain your ankle if the idea upsets you."

"I shall endeavour to bear up," he muttered, and there was a decided gleam in his eyes as he took her hands for the final bars of the leaping, twirling measure.

The fiddlers scraped to a triumphant finish, the dancers dipped and swayed into the embrace that ended their leaps and circling, each gentleman leaning to kiss his partner. Abigail half closed her eyes as Paget seized her.

For an instant that hung like a jewel on the links of Time she was warm submission in his arms. Then his teeth bit into her lips, forcing them apart, his tongue thrusting into her mouth, his breath hot and swift, drawing the last resistance out of her body. Long shudders ran through her limbs and the yearning was a blind hunger that cared nothing for honour or affection, but sought only its own satisfaction. If he had taken her then, in the midst of them all, she would not even have wanted to resist him.

But the music had begun again and he was handing her over to a merry-eyed gentleman with red hair. His voice seemed to come from a vast distance. "You met Peter Mainwaring earlier, my love. When we were boys he was a notable dancer, as I remember."

"When our elders were not looking," the other said. "Both our fathers considered we were a bad influence on each other."

"I fear I am a bad influence on anybody," Paget said. "Isn't that so, Abigail?"

His eyes and smile were triumphant. He had noticed her response and was openly glorying in it. She would have given anything to remove that triumph from his handsome, confident face, but he had bowed and moved away, and her new partner was leading her into the set.

The new dance was a more complicated one, in which partners were frequently changed as the pattern shifted and the ladies linked hands circling the kneeling gentlemen. Abigail went through the steps automatically, smiling, dipping, swaying at the right times, her mind not a thousand miles away but across the room where Paget was talking to John Bailey.

"May I get you a glass of wine? You look a little flushed." Peter Mainwaring was talking to her. Abigail dragged her mind back to him with an effort, blinking into his pleasant, freckled face.

"I beg your pardon?"

"I was asking if you would like a glass of wine, but your thoughts were upon other matters."

"I'm sorry, you must think me very rude. Yes, wine would be lovely," she said hastily.

Paget was dancing again with a little, faded woman who giggled all the time. Resolutely she turned her gaze away from him and allowed Peter Mainwaring to escort her back to the hall. The dishes had been cleared, but decanters of wine and bowls of nuts and fruit were set out on the table. He poured wine for them both and began to chat about the other guests, pointing them out to her as they drifted through.

"Julia Sawyer earns her living as a governess now. Before the war she was one of the most eligible girls in the county, but her family lost everything. You will like Mistress Sawyer. Paget has bestowed a small annuity on her, so that when she retires she will not be left destitute – but you will know about that already."

"Paget doesn't always make his private charities known," she murmured.

"And would be furious if they were spoken about. He doesn't wear his heart on his sleeve, save where you're concerned."

"Me?" She looked up at him in surprise.

" 'Tis clear that he is head over heels in love with you. I never saw a man so besotted with a maiden."

"He does give that appearance," she murmured.

"But I must confess some surprise," he admitted, "I would have thought that he would have found a wife in France. But instead he came into his inheritance and took an English rose instead of a foreign flower."

"You did not go into exile," she said.

"My father was of a Puritan cast of thought," he said wryly. "He was able to keep our home, though we ran it on a somewhat reduced income. I am myself more adaptable than Paget. I didn't mind living under the Protectorate, but Paget would not have endured it. He was always one to speak his mind, and that got us into trouble when we were lads!"

"With Uncle Henry Delaney? I met him once, years ago, and he was very stern and cold."

"He was a man who firmly believed that he was always right and other people were nearly always wrong. A ruthless man," Peter Mainwaring said thoughtfully.

'And Paget is ruthless too,' Abigail thought. 'He is determined to get what he wants.'

"Are you cold, mistress?" her companion asked. "You shivered."

"A goose on my grave," she said, draining her glass.

"Will you dance again?" he asked.

"No, I think I ought to mingle with some of the other guests, else they will think me ill-mannered," she decided.

"If anyone did dare to hold such an opinion I would call them out and challenge them to a duel," Peter Mainwaring vowed.

"And spoil the party? Save your energies for the dancing," she advised, laughing.

"But not with you? So be it, but I'll claim a dance again before the evening is done." He bowed over her hand and strolled away towards the dancers.

Dusk was darkening into night and the first pale stars were peppering the sky. Those who were not dancing or drinking had wandered into the parlour where cards and chess had been set up for those who preferred to sit in quieter comfort. The servants had replenished the fires and the house was warm, the smoke of the logs and of the many candles rising blue-grey to the high ceiling. One or two of the guests smiled as they passed her. A gentleman paused to compliment her on the excellence of the supper.

There was no sign of Paget. She knew that almost without having to look for him. When Paget entered a room he brought with him an intense, exciting quality. When he was with her she felt, not always peaceful or happy, but more fiercely alive, conscious of the varying emotions within her. When he was absent everything seemed muted and colourless. Wistfully she thought how marvellous it would be if he truly loved her.

The main door stood open for after the cool of the day

the evening was warm. Abigail went out to the steps and stood for a few moments, breathing in the perfume of the night-scented stock that grew beneath the windows and edged the lawn. Against the sky the shaped yews were like sentinels.

Perhaps, after all, she had been mistaken in her handling of the situation. Perhaps he did love her after his fashion and she, through hurt pride, had driven a wedge between them. Thoughtfully she descended the steps and wandered across the grass, her head bent. There were stone benches set at intervals in the garden. She sat down on one, the thought crossing her mind that perhaps her own mother had once sat in this place and dreamed of escaping from her harsh elder brother.

"I tell you I'll not endure it much longer."

The vehement whisper startled Abigail. It came from behind a nearby clump of bushes and the voice was Henrietta's. She was certain of that even before she heard Paget's reply.

"Another week or two, and we'll tell her. I promise you."

"I feel so guilty," Henrietta was complaining. "She is a pleasant person and what we're doing is unfair."

"When one is in love there are excuses," Paget said. "But I'll not keep the truth hidden much longer. We agreed on a time limit."

"Every time I look at her I want to confess the whole matter," Henrietta said. "It seems so cheap and shabby to deceive her."

"Not for much longer." Paget's low voice was reassuring. "She is in love with me already, I believe, but will not admit it. Only let her acknowledge the fact and she'll not object. And that can only profit you."

Their voices died, and the rustling of a skirt

betokened a withdrawal. Abigail sat rigidly on the bench, her fists clenched, her brown eyes wide with shocked anger. So what she had suspected from the moment Paget had brought Henrietta into the house was true. The blonde, blue-eyed housekeeper was his mistress, and Paget believed that once Abigail had fallen in love with him she would make no objections to the relationship. No doubt he had visions of them living as a happy threesome, in defiance of every moral and honourable code.

She was so angry that she felt physically sick. And at the core of her fury was a loneliness of spirit because, though she would die before admitting it, she could no longer disguise from herself the fact that she had fallen in love with the man she had married. It had happened against her will and despite his behaviour, and knowing the truth about him had not altered her feelings one jot. She despised him as much as she desired him, and she hated herself for her own weakness.

She was not sure how long she had sat staring into the darkness, but her hands were very cold, and her head had begun to ache. She rose and walked back slowly to the house. The musicians in the gallery were eating their belated supper, and from the long drawing room the notes of the spinet tinkled out.

Henrietta was playing, her fair head bent over the keys, and Paget stood near, an appreciative smile on his lips. Many of the guests stood around listening to the melody. Abigail stood rigidly within the door, her eyes burning into Henrietta's back. The scene was so intimate, so charming, the brown and gold of Paget's suit blending with the ivory and gold of Henrietta's gown.

The melody tinkled to its end and there was a hearty round of applause. Abigail found herself walking forwards, a smile on her face, her voice cool and high.

"That was a most creditable performance, my dear. I'm sure our guests will excuse you if you return to your duties now. Paget, will you tell Robin that we require more wine? We like to keep the best until last."

Henrietta had flushed to the roots of her hairline and Paget's face was like stone. Abigail ignored them both, turning to John Bailey with her hands outstretched.

"You have not danced with me, Master Bailey! The musicians will start to play again in a few minutes and then we shall see how our steps match! But first we must drink a toast to His Majesty! Were it not for his restoration to the throne we would not be having such a wonderful time!"

Paget turned on his heel and walked away. She saw his eyes brilliant as steel, and something within her quivered. Then she was laughing and talking again, urging them all to fill their goblets.

"To King Charles the Second, God bless him."

It was Mark Griffin who gave the toast and all about her glasses were raised.

"The King, God bless him!"

The wine was honey on her lips but vinegar as she swallowed it and saw Paget, his arm about Henrietta's shoulders in a brief, comforting embrace. Then the young woman slipped away and Paget strolled forward, lifting his glass.

"To my one true love," he said, his eyes on Abigail's face, his lips curled in the enigmatic smile which she was beginning to learn masked anger.

The music began again and John Bailey came politely to claim his dance. After that there was Peter Mainwaring, and a gentleman called Donald Ray, and then another gentleman whose name she couldn't catch. She danced more and more gaily, laughing and talking as she leapt and whirled, her cheeks flushed, despair leaden in the pit of her stomach.

The horses and a small coach for three elderly ladies had been brought round to the front. Abigail stood at the door, shaking hands with the departing guests. Paget stood with her, his voice cordial as he received their thanks for an excellent evening. Behind them the great hall with its wilting flowers and litter of dirty glasses had a deserted air.

"Will you be coming to the fair tomorrow, mistress?" John Bailey asked as he took his leave.

As she hesitated Paget broke in, his voice smooth.

"I'm sure Abigail will be there if she is not too exhausted after this evening."

"I shall look forward to it," she said.

The hall was empty now and the air blowing from the darkness struck chill on her bare shoulders. Without looking at Paget she turned and went upstairs.

A fire had been lit in her bedroom and the quilt had been turned back invitingly. Abigail sank into a chair and rested her aching head in her hands. At that moment she wanted only to be let alone, but the closing of the door signalled Paget's arrival.

CHAPTER ELEVEN

He had cast off both jacket and smile and his face was grim. The door closed, he stood with his back against it, glaring at her with such intensity that she inwardly quailed. "I'm waiting," he said.

"Are you indeed." She schooled her own face and voice to indifference. "May I ask what you're expecting?"

"An explanation," Paget said, "of your unkindness to Henrietta."

"My – unkindness to Henrietta! You think I was unkind?"

"You made it very clear that you considered her to be a servant."

"Oh, then I beg both your pardons!" she retorted. "I ought to have made it clear that I considered her to be your mistress!"

For a moment, watching the vein in his temple swell, she feared that he was going to strike her. Then, by some effort of will, he relaxed, lifting one black eyebrow quizzically as he moved towards her.

"And how did you reach that conclusion, my love?" he enquired.

"I guessed," she said lamely, unwilling to admit that she had eavesdropped.

"And displayed your jealousy in a rather ill-disciplined manner," he said.

"Ill-disciplined!" She echoed the word indignantly.

"By leaping like a wanton with every Tom, Dick and Harry in the room!"

"I danced!" she said in amazement. "Since when has a Royalist considered it a crime to dance?"

"Laughing and jesting with other men, as if you had forgotten your married state!"

"I am your wife in name only," she said icily. "And my dancing and jesting is as nothing compared to your lechery."

"Of which you've no proof beyond your own suspicions," he interrupted.

"I'm not a complete fool," Abigail said.

"And do you object?" He spoke slowly and there was a look on his face that was hard to analyse. "Do you object to my making love to Henrietta?"

"The scandal—" she began, but he interrupted her again, his eyes on her face.

"There is no scandal, nor will there be. I speak of your own feelings. Does it offend you to think of Henrietta Brown and me together?

For a moment she wanted to cry out that no picture hurt her more deeply than the one her mind had painted of him fondling the blonde housekeeper. She wanted to tell him that, wager or no wager, she loved him and would submit. But if she did then the last shreds of her self-respect would be gone, and she could imagine his triumph at having worn down her resistance.

"For myself I've no interest in your love affairs," she said coldly. "Satisfy your lusts where you please, but have the decency to be discreet about it."

He gave her a brief, bitter smile and walked out without answering. She had won and the threatened scene had been averted. Paget Delaney would not come to her room again. They would live as polite strangers, one never questioning the other, and no doubt he'd make certain there was no scandal.

Abigail had not submitted, and yet her triumph tasted of defeat. Huddled in the chair by the glowing fire, she knew without a shadow of doubt that she would never be able to endure the dismal years ahead. To be a wife in name only, with all her young promise blighted, was a dreadful prospect, made even worse by the fact that she would be living in the same house as the man she desired. It would be better if she never saw him again. As she had never consummated her marriage then surely it could be annulled? She had heard that such a thing was possible but she had no idea how to go about it.

Thomas Wellborn came into her mind. Thomas was a lawyer and would be able to help her. Indeed he would be pleased to help her, she was certain. She was equally certain that Paget would never allow her to seek an annullment. She would have to leave Delaney Court in secret and ask Thomas to begin the necessary proceedings. Neither could she risk going back to Lane House, for her father, seeing the loss of his pension, would certainly force her to return to Paget. She felt no remorse at the thought of his losing his pension through her action, for he had sold her into the marriage with no consideration for her happiness.

It was ironic, she thought, that she had been prepared to live in enmity with a husband she disliked, but could not bear the same situation now that she realised she was in love.

A sob rose in her throat and her eyes stung with tears, but she blinked them back and began to plan.

The next morning she came down to a hall flooded

with sunshine. Everything had been swept and cleared, and a genial bustle prevailed in the kitchen as the servants got ready for the fair.

"It's a lovely day, mistress," Lettice said, hurrying up with a tray in her hands. "I slept late this morning, but your breakfast's ready."

"I'll have it in the parlour," Abigail said, taking the tray from her. "You go and get yourself ready for the Fair. Tell cook we'll have something cold later, and she's to go and enjoy herself with the others."

"Yes, mistress." Lettice bobbed a curtsy and went back into the kitchen. Abigail carried the tray through to the parlour and set it on the table. The fire had not been lit and a pack of cards was scattered over the couch. She began to gather them up, then stiffened as Henrietta came in. The housekeeper wore the blue dress she had worn on her arrival, but she looked tired and a little depressed.

With a little shock of surprise Abigail realised that the situation could scarcely be a comfortable one for Henrietta either. There had been real desperation in her voice the previous night.

"I beg your pardon, Mistress Abigail, but I've not attended to this room yet," she said.

Abigail forced herself to speak pleasantly. This would, with luck, be the last time she would have any contact with Paget's mistress.

"You go along to the fair. This can wait until later."

"There was something I wanted to say," Henrietta said, twisting her hands together. "I've kept silent a long time but now I feel I have to speak out."

"Not now, Henrietta!" Abigail's voice was sharp. The last thing she wanted at that moment was a tearful confession from her husband's lover.

"But you ought to know—"

"Not *now*! We'll talk later on tonight." Abigail sat down and began to eat her cooling breakfast with a calmness that masked her turmoil of feelings. Henrietta bit her lip, then reluctantly withdrew.

'By tonight,' Abigail thought, 'I'll be on my way to Thomas, and she may have Paget and the house.'

She was not certain how she would contrive to reach Thomas. If she took the Windsor road she would probably be able to hire an escort to ride with her the rest of the way. She knew where Thomas lodged and she had no doubt he would help her. The marriage that was no marriage would be quietly ended by due process of law, and then she and Thomas would be wed and probably sail to the New World out of reach of Paget's vengeance and her father's anger. It was the perfect ending and, when she contemplated it, she felt more utterly miserable than she had ever felt in her life.

"The horses for the coach are come, so we can ride in state to the Fair," Paget announced, coming in. He looked handsome and vigorous, and her hand shook as she put down her tankard.

"I have a slight headache," she said, "so I think I'll stay at home today."

"The air will do you good," he said. "You've not a scrap of colour in your face. Anyway, you cannot possibly stay here all alone."

"I shall be perfectly safe," she said obstinately.

"But with a mysterious stranger hanging around—"

"The vapourings of an hysterical maid!" she snapped, irritated by the setback to her plans. "I doubt if anyone saw anything. I would prefer to stay at home."

"And I would prefer you to come." He had set his jaw and his eyes glittered.

"Then you may drag me there," she said sweetly. "That will set all the tongues wagging, 'tis certain."

"Stay, then." His voice was curt as he turned on his heel.

It was foolish, but she couldn't bear it to end between them on a note of anger. This was the last time they would ever be alone together, and she was childish enough to want some happy memory in the years to come.

"Paget, I do wish you a happy day," she said wistfully.

"Do you?" His long searching look penetrated to her heart. Then he raised his eyebrow in the familiar cynical look, said very gently, "Thank you, my dear," and withdrew.

The room was very cold despite the sunshine pouring through the windows and the bacon on her plate looked greasy and unappetising. She pushed it away and sat with bowed head, listening to the jangle of harness and the rattling of wheels as the household prepared to leave. It was not yet ten o'clock, and she guessed they wouldn't return until after dusk.

There were some coins in a carved box on the side. She counted them out frowningly. Twelve guineas would surely hire her an escort and buy bed and board along the road, and Thomas would lend her whatever else was needed. Dear, kind Thomas with his steady blue eyes and equally steady principles! She fixed her mind on their reunion, pushing aside the image of a lean, dark face, glittering grey eyes, and black hair that fell thick and shining about his broad shoulders.

The coins in her purse, she rose and went out into the hall. The quietness of the house settled about her. This was the first time she had been alone here, and for a moment she wished that she had the leisure to wander through its vast apartments and savour the pleasure of being mistress. But that would be stupid when she was on the verge of leaving.

She went through to the kitchen, which had an unfamiliar air with ashes raked over the coals and the table scrubbed and bare. The servants had all gone now, but the echoes of their gossip seemed to hang in the air. They would certainly whisper together when they discovered she had gone. Paget would hate that, for she sensed that his pride was great. Well, it would do him no harm to have that pride dented by servants' chatter.

Slowly she came back into the hall and began to mount the stairs. Last evening she and Paget had walked down together to greet the neighbours. They must have looked the very picture of a devoted couple. She pushed the memory away and tried to concentrate on her immediate plans. She would put on her plain dress and her russet cloak, leave her emerald betrothal ring behind, and ride out on Cora. If she took the forest path she would be able to get clear of Delaney land without being seen.

On the way to her room she hesitated. Paget's bedroom was down the corridor. She had never actually been into the room, and she had no clear idea why she wanted to go there now, but the impulse was so strong that she went on past her own door and entered the apartment.

It was a dim, cold chamber with a narrow bed and the dark hangings that had once hung also in the lower apartments. There was nothing here of Paget's personality, nothing but the silence of an empty unattractive room. And Paget had taken this dismal apartment while she had enjoyed the comfort of the room he had prepared especially for her. Or had he gone every night to Henrietta's bedroom? There was nothing here to answer her question, nothing to remind her of Paget.

"But I don't wish to be reminded of him," she muttered furiously. "He wed me only to dishonour me."

'And you married him because you were not brave enough to stand out against everybody,' a small voice insisted. 'You married him, and then you refused to be a real wife. If he cheated you about the wager, then you cheated him too because your pride was hurt. You never even tried to make him love you.'

She put her hands over her ears to shut out that small insistent voice, but it went on without pause.

'You just don't love Thomas Wellborn. He was just a habit that you outgrew a long time ago. You love Paget but you won't admit it. You expect him to be perfect, but he's just a man, a faulty human being. And you could have made him love you, if only you had forgotten your pride and shown your true feelings.'

It was too late for regrets. She had lost her courage once, but she was resolved not to lose it again. This last hour at Delaney Court would be painful, but the pain would fade in time, and she would be free of the strange, wild emotions that tore through her.

There was a noise, a soft footfall, that brought her back to the present moment with a jerk. For a moment she thought she had imagined it, but then the noise came again more distinctly. She went to the door and looked down the corridor just in time to see the door of her own apartment softly close.

Terror gripped her at the realisation that she was alone and far from any possible help. The sensible course of action would be to steal quietly past, down the main staircase, through to the stables where she could mount Cora and ride away. If thieves had taken this opportunity to ransack the house, it was none of her concern. But they were in her room, in the apartment that Paget had had decorated for her arrival. Gritting her teeth she moved towards the door, wishing she had a gun or a knife, or a heavy candlestick with which she had a vague idea of hitting somebody over the head.

With the door closed she could hear nothing, but her instincts told her that she hadn't been mistaken. Someone was in that room, moving stealthily, touching her things with alien fingers. Anger overcame fear, and she flung wide the door.

Two men swung around and stared at her. Obviously they were not thieves. Thieves didn't wear handsome satin jackets and puffed breeches and short, velvet cloaks, or carry dress swords. Nonplussed, Abigail gaped at them both.

The taller of the two men was the first to recover his composure. He stepped forward, bowing, pulling off his feathered hat. "Mistress Abigail Delaney? We thought you gone to the Fair with the rest of the household."

"Evidently!" She advanced into the room, looking round in dismay at the scattered ornaments and cushions. "What gives you the right to come in here and behave as if you own the place? *Who are you*?"

"Master Trybinn, mistress. This is Master Penhallow."

"I've never heard of either of you," she said coldly.

"We serve his majesty King Charles," Master Trybinn said.

"Breaking into other people's houses? Is that one of your duties?" she asked.

"Sometimes it is a regrettable necessity, mistress."

"A necessity! How dare you seek to justify your impudence in such a manner? When is it *necessary* to invade people's privacy in such a fashion?"

"When treason is suspected," he said.

"Treason?" The colour draining from her face, she sat down abruptly on the end of the bed. "Treason?"

"Suspicion of it, mistress."

"In this house? You must be mistaken," Abigail whispered.

"Information has been laid, and we were bidden to make enquiries."

"You were searching!" she accused. "And that man is still searching, turning out the cupboards! Make him stop!"

"He's only doing his duty, mistress."

"When my husband returns he'll have you both horsewhipped!" she cried furiously.

"Master Trybinn, I think we have what we were seeking," the one called Penhallow said.

He had straightened up with a small, flat packet in his hand. Master Trybinn went over to him and there was the ripping of paper as they bent over their find.

"Look, will you please tell me what's happening?" Abigail said. "What in the world is going on?"

"An excellent question, my dear," Paget said from the open door. "I am probably even more interested in the answer than you are. I made an excuse to ride back, expecting to find you with one gentleman, and I find you with two. I hope that you have an explanation, sirs." His voice was casual but his eyes were steely.

"Master Delaney?" The tall man had come forward and was bowing.

"You have the advantage of me," Paget said.

"James Trybinn, sir, and this is my colleague, Christopher Penhallow. I have been watching the house for some time."

So there had been someone in the garden that night!

"For what reason?" Paget asked.

"Information was laid," Master Trybinn said, "telling us that a treasonable plot was being laid at Delaney Court. A plot to kill the King, sir, on his way to his coronation."

"And you imagine that someone in this household would be party to such a thing? You must be out of your mind!" Paget said flatly.

"We have the evidence, sir. A list of the conspirators with your own name to head the list, plans of the coronation route, money to be offered in bribes to those guards who might agree to leave the King undefended. It is all here, Master Delaney."

But it was all wrong! The package that Master Penhallow was holding was the one that Thomas Wellborn had given to her, telling her to open it at Yuletide.

"Where were these papers found?" Paget asked.

"At the bottom of the chest, sir, under the linen," Master Penhallow said. "Under Mistress Delaney's shifts and petticoats, sir."

"My lady wife knows nothing of it," Paget said, without looking at her.

"Then you admit the papers were hidden here by you, sir?"

"I admit nothing." Paget's face was still averted, his voice cold and clipped. "I have the right to refuse to speak."

"It is my duty to arrest you, sir, in the name of the King." The tall man sounded almost apologetic.

"I will make no resistance." Calmly Paget unbuckled

his sword and laid it down. "My lady wife will inform the rest of my household what has occurred when they return from the Fair. Do we ride to London?"

"Aye, sir. You will be lodged in the Tower for further questioning. These names are unfamiliar to us."

"And I can tell you nothing about them," Paget said scornfully.

"You've not looked at the list yet, sir," the other pointed out.

"I don't need to look at it, there is nothing to tell."

"Then we'll leave quietly, sir. You are in good health and don't suffer from hernia?"

Abigail saw the muscles of his jaw tighten but he answered placidly. "I am in splendid health and never suffered a serious ailment in my life."

"With your permission then, Master Delaney."

Paget bowed and walked out, his bearing as untroubled as if he had been invited to a supper party. He had not looked at her once, but she knew that he had been intensely aware of her during the whole bizarre conversation.

"I regret the shock this must be, Mistress Delaney," Master Penhallow said, lingering with a look of sympathy on his face.

"There's a mistake," she said dully. "There's been a terrible mistake."

"I hope so, mistress." He had turned to follow the others but her voice, tight with strain, recalled him.

"Why did Master Trybinn enquire about my husband's health?"

"It is forbidden to put a man suffering from hernia to the question," he said.

"The ques –? Do you mean the *rack*?" Eyes wide with horror, she stared at him.

"It may not be necessary," he began.

"Necessary! Torture is illegal," she cried.

"Official torture is illegal," he agreed, "but in cases of treason, certain rules may be relaxed at the discretion of the Council. Your pardon, mistress, but we cannot delay any further."

It wasn't happening. Somehow or other she must have fallen asleep and dreamed horribly. Abigail closed her eyes briefly, shuddering, then opened them upon the disorder of her apartment. It was reality, and no dream. From beyond the window she could hear the chinking of harness. Her legs shook as she crossed to look out. The three men were mounting their horses, and for an instant as she stood there Paget raised his eyes to the casement above. Even at a distance she shrank from their blazing contempt.

The riders diminished into the distance and were lost among the trees. Abigail strained her eyes after them until they were hidden from view. She felt cold and sick, and more bewildered than she had ever been.

Paget had been arrested for treason, and he had not troubled to deny it. He had ridden away without a word to her. Yet he must have realised that the package belonged to her. And that meant that he believed she was the one who plotted treason.

But he had chosen to take the blame himself, to risk possible torture and death. With the restoration of the King feelings of revenge against those who had kept him in exile for eleven years were running high. No mercy would be shown to anyone suspected of treason, and if Paget refused to speak there was no hope for him at all.

Abigail shivered, thinking of that proud, dark face contorted in pain, the graceful limbs broken on the rack. Paget would never tell the truth, she was certain. He would never blame her in public, though in private he must surely detest her. His final glance up at the window had shown that.

And yet he had gone silently to what might well prove his death, and that death would be more horrible to her than her own.

CHAPTER TWELVE

It was evening when Henrietta and Lettice arrived back from the Fair. They looked flushed and happily tired, small bags of lavender and sweetmeats in their arms. Robin was with them and other members of the household, the maids perched on a hay-wain, were making their way across the fields.

"Mistress, you ought to have come!" Lettice exclaimed. "We had a splendid time! Oh, it was not to be compared to the big Fairs that used to be held when I was a girl, but it was marvellous to see folks enjoying themselves."

Her voice trailed into silence as she caught sight of Abigail who stood at the foot of the stairs, her hand clenched about the newel post, her mouth compressed into a straight line that revealed, rather than hid, the long hours of anguish she had spent.

"What is it? Are you ill?" Henrietta asked, hurrying towards her.

"Come into the parlour, Henrietta. I have to talk to you. Lettice, tell the others to start their supper."

Without waiting for an answer she went across the hall into the apartment. Neither fire nor candles had been lit, and the room was almost in darkness.

"Shall I light the candles?" Henrietta asked, closing the door.

"Yes, the tinder box is on the side." Abigail tried to keep her voice steady.

The candles flared into light and Henrietta exclaimed in dismay at the other's chalk-white face and haunted eyes.

"You're ill, mistress! Oh, I knew that we ought not to have left you alone!"

"I'm perfectly well," Abigail said stiffly. "Paget –"

"He came back lest you'd changed your mind and I haven't seen him all day."

"Paget has been arrested," Abigail said.

"Arrested? For what reason?" Henrietta asked blankly.

"High treason," Abigail said flatly.

"High – treason! Mistress, you must be wrong. Nobody is more loyal to his majesty than Pag – Master Paget!"

"You may drop the pretence," Abigail said. "I know about it now."

"He told you? Oh, I hoped that he would, even if it is a disadvantage to my own future, but Paget is so kind he will find a means of making it up to me. But he can't have been arrested! It's not possible!"

"He has been taken to the Tower," Abigail said, and burst into the racking sobs she had been holding back all day. Henrietta, with great tact, sat motionless until the storm had subsided. Then, very quietly, all pretence of being a servant fled, she said,

"My dear, please try to be calm and tell me exactly what happened. You say Paget has been arrested?"

Abigail nodded, dabbing at her eyes miserably. "Two men came here," she said, "and found a list of names, and plans for the killing of the King. When Paget came in they arrested him, and he would say nothing."

"But where did the list come from?"

It was the question that Abigail had been dreading. She drew a deep breath and spoke honestly. "The list was given to me by a friend of mine. I didn't know what it contained. I know that sounds odd, but it's true."

"But couldn't you have said so? Why didn't Paget tell them he knew nothing of it?"

"Because he believed me guilty, I suppose, and his honour would not allow him to betray me. How can I tell what Paget Delaney thinks about anything?"

"How could he believe you guilty, if you didn't know what was in the list?" Henrietta asked, puzzled.

"I didn't tell him about the package I was given," Abigail said.

"Oh, I see."

"No, you don't see!" Abigail sprang up and began to pace the room restlessly. "You have never tried to see how it has been for me, married against my will for the sake of a wager—"

"That stupid wager! I told them both it was foolish and dishonourable."

"You knew of it before?"

"In France, when none of us had any money," Henrietta said, "Paget believed that his father had carried out his threat to disinherit him, and he declared that when he did come home he'd pay the old man out by wedding his cousin Abigail. Paul Kenton declared that he'd never bring you to it, and they made the wager."

"So if I fell in love with him then he would win. He used me."

"He wanted to win your affection," Henrietta said.

"By bringing you here? By flaunting his mistress?"

"But you said he'd explained!"

"That you were his mistress? He didn't need to

explain that! I guessed it a long time ago, and when he wrote to you—"

"Wrote to me?" The blue eyes were wide.

"Don't act the innocent!" Abigail snapped. "I saw you hide away a letter on the morning the post boy came."

"This letter?" Henrietta took it from her little draw-string pocket.

"You always carry it with you, I see!" Abigail gibed.

"Read it," Henrietta said, thrusting the letter at her. "Read it!"

Unwillingly Abigail took it. 'My own darling' leapt at her from the paper, and the other lines blurred and ran together. He had called her his own darling, and jealousy caught her in its grip, tossing her to and fro. She forced herself to concentrate on the words, bracing herself against the expected pain.

'My own darling,

'A brief line to assure you I am in good health but low in spirits, because it seems so long since we were together and you lay in my arms. I am not certain when our love-sick friend intends to return to Delaney Court, so will entrust this to the post boy rather than to him. I wish you could tell me about the surprise that you're planning, but Paget assures me that all will be well and our marriage can take place very soon. The day cannot be too soon for me, my sweet. My kindest regards to Mistress Abigail and to dear, faithful Lettice.

'To you, dearest Henrietta,

'My devoted Love,

'Paul.'

Paul! The name Paul was so totally unexpected that she had to go back to the beginning again because the letter made no sense. None of it made any sense.

"Paul Kenton and I have been in love for a long time," Henrietta said, "but I would not marry him without dowry. Then Paget came to see me. He said you disliked him and had refused to bed with him, and he asked me to help him win the wager."

"To take money from the man you loved?"

"Paget promised that money to me as a dowry if I could succeed in making you jealous," Henrietta confessed. "I was unwilling, but Paget was very anxious for you to be true wife to him, and he believed the plan might work. We intended to tell you. I wanted him to tell you, for in helping him I began to fear that I might compromise my own reputation."

"And Paul Kenton doesn't know?"

Henrietta shook her blonde head. "Paul thinks I'm here as housekeeper. We were going to tell him later, of course. And now, it's all gone awry. Paget is taken for treason because a friend of yours gave you something, and the wager failed anyway. Paget told me this morning when we set out for the Fair that he believed you really hated him."

"But didn't you realise that he hadn't explained matters to me?" Abigail asked.

"He didn't say anything about that," Henrietta said. "He simply told me that you hated him, but he was coming back to make one last attempt."

"And when he walked in the two men were already here." Abigail gave back the letter and sat down. She had not eaten all day, and was beginning to feel slightly light-headed, but the picture was clear now. Out of a comedy of errors had come a potential tragedy. "Paget was determined to win his wager, wasn't he?" she said bitterly.

"Well, he knows now that his belief was right," Henrietta said. "You really do hate him."

"How do you know what I feel?" Abigail demanded.

"Why, you let him be taken for treason instead of confessing your own part in it," Henrietta returned.

Her voice was accusing and the sympathy had gone from her face. Abigail wanted to protest that everything had happened so fast that she'd had no time to think, no time to understand why Paget should silently take the blame, but it would not have been the whole truth. The whole truth was that some part of her had wanted to hurt and punish him because of his attentions to Henrietta.

"It may not be as bad as we fear," the other said. "The King knows Paget to be loyal, and Paul is still at Court and will surely speak for him."

But they had taken Paget to the Tower and the King was still at Whitehall, and might not even know of the arrest yet. Meanwhile, if Paget remained silent and was put to the question – her mind shrank from that possibility.

"I will speak for him myself," she said. "First thing in the morning we'll go to Whitehall and beg audience of the King. I'll make him believe that Paget is loyal."

"Then you'll involve yourself, and your – friend," Henrietta said.

"I'll think of something," Abigail was beginning when there was a tap at the door and Lettice came in.

"I brought some supper," she said, her eyes moving inquisitively between them.

"Lettice, did you know that Mistress Henrietta was betrothed to Master Kenton?" Abigail asked.

The maidservant shot a quick glance at Henrietta and nodded slowly. "I've only known since Mistress Henrietta came here," she said. "I tell you frankly that I haven't approved at all, mistress. 'Tis not fair of any of you to be play-acting and pretending. But Master Paget said he was going to tell you all about it very soon, and it wasn't really my place to speak out. I was wondering where he is and if he needs any supper?"

"Master Paget has been called away on business," Abigail said quickly. "I won't need you again tonight, so you can go to bed whenever you choose."

"Yes, mistress." Lettice bobbed a curtsy and went out.

"You said *we* would go to Court?" Henrietta queried, handing Abigail some sliced chicken.

"You will like to see Paul Kenton;" Abigail said. "Robin can escort us."

"And you really mean to see the King?"

"I'll seek audience," Abigail said firmly. "I'll make the King listen to me."

She spoke bravely, but her heart was sinking lower with each moment that passed. By now Paget would be well on the way to the Tower, if not already there. Abigail had never visited London, but she had heard tales of the grim fortress where state prisoners were kept. The thought that Paget Delaney might, at this very moment, be in one of the cold dungeons was more than she could endure. The supper that Lettice had prepared tasted of nothing, but she forced it down, knowing that she needed something if she were to keep up her strength.

"If you had ridden to the Fair," Henrietta was reproaching, "we could have started out today."

"I had to think," Abigail said vaguely.

She had tried to think, but instead she had sat, hour after hour, staring into the emptiness of the room until its loneliness filled her entire being. "I think I'll go for a walk," she said abruptly, pushing her plate away. "I need some air."

"Shall I come with you?" Henrietta asked.

"No, I prefer to be alone." Abigail spoke curtly. She was aware that Henrietta regarded her with a certain amount of critical suspicion, but she'd no intention of confiding in her further.

It was cool and fresh in the garden. She walked slowly to the end of the drive, remembering against her will how she had first ridden on to Delaney land in a mood of sullen resentment because she had been married for a wager. If she had not overheard that conversation between Paget and Paul at the inn she would never have known the truth, and none of this might have happened.

"Abigail! Mistress Abigail!"

The low voice came from the trees at her right. She swung round as Thomas Wellborn stepped out.

"Thomas? I thought you long gone," she began in confusion, but he interrupted, seizing her hands between his.

"It was reckless, I know, but I had to come back, to see if all went as planned. It was beyond my hopes that you might come out here tonight."

"Paget has been arrested for high treason," she said.

"I saw them ride away," he told her. "They found the package then with the list of names and the plan? I told them he would probably have hidden it among your possessions."

"You told them?" But some part of her had known it all the time.

"It was not easy," Thomas said, "to write to those who would act on the information in an anonymous letter. But I took a chance, hoping the information I gave would be investigated."

"But he is known to be loyal," Abigail said.

"Nobody is above suspicion," Thomas said. "Charles Stuart must be aware that not everyone is delighted at his restoration, and Paget Delaney will be hard put to it to prove his innocence."

"The names on the list—"

"All invented. Nobody else will be involved, and you need have no fears for yourself. Your parents will make it clear that you were forced to marry."

"If Paget is found guilty he will be executed," she said, dry-mouthed.

"That will be unfortunate, for I always abhorred violence," Thomas said regretfully. "But Paget Delaney did not consider the feelings of anybody but himself when he married you."

She said nothing, but went on staring at him in the darkness.

"I am more pleased than I can say to be able to talk to you. I had thoughts of trying to see you, but feared lest any suspicion of collusion fell upon you," he was continuing. "No harm must come to you, my betrothed."

"Betrothed?" Her voice was a whisper.

"I never thought of you as anything else," he said earnestly. "You will be Paget Delaney's widow soon, and then we can be married. Delaney Court will be our home."

"Delaney Court?"

"You will inherit," he reminded her. "Oh, as the law stands a third of the property of a condemned traitor is forfeit to the Crown, but we can sell off some of the land

and still have a goodly estate. I made certain of the fact before I laid my plan."

"That was – far-seeing of you," she murmured.

"My dear, I wouldn't be a very good lawyer if I didn't think ahead," he said smilingly. "You must have no fears for our future together, but that future has to be delayed. We cannot risk being seen together. But I will think of you often, very often."

He drew her closer and bent, his lips cool on her cheek. Shudders of revulsion went through her, but his low voice was unsuspicious.

"You need not fear for my safety or your own. Go back to the house now before you are missed. I am lodging at the Crown and Anchor near Windsor, under the name of Giles Armitage. I'll stay on for a couple of days in the hostelry lest you wish to contact me urgently and then I'll ride home. It's best if we don't meet or write for a few months. It's hard, I know, but I am a patient man."

Very patient, she thought, to have planned such a scheme, and very sure of her feelings to be so certain that she'd let Paget be executed for treason without saying one word to clear him.

"My affection for you is unchanged," he was saying.

She supposed that, according to his own standards, he was telling the truth. He had not loved her enough to fling away his career on her behalf, but when she was a widow and owned the estate then he would resume his interrupted courtship, and she had no doubt he would be a very faithful husband.

Gently she disengaged herself, whispering, "You'd best leave."

"For not too long, if all goes according to plan." He kissed her cheek again and went softly away.

She had known, of course, that it had been Thomas Wellborn who had laid the plan and sent the false information. But this was the first time she had realised the cold calculation that was part of his nature. Paget had shamed her by the wager, but he surely didn't deserve to die for it!

Walking back to the house, Abigail knew that she was left with no choice. Whatever the outcome, she could not stand by and let Paget be executed for a crime he had not committed. What was absolutely certain was that Paget would never forgive her, or look at her again with desire in his eyes, and she would never know if that desire had been for herself or simply to win his wager.

Her room was still in disorder. She lit the candles and looked round, remembering how bright and luxurious it had looked in contrast to the rest of the house when she had first arrived. Only three months before and she seemed to have lived a lifetime since then. Now the house was warmly welcoming and she had learned to dance. With an almost physical pain the memory of that recent supper party returned. Had it really been only the previous night that he had looked at her with glad surprise because she was so light of foot? And if she had not misunderstood those few sentences exchanged between Henrietta and Paget, the evening might have had a very different ending. The bed with its rumpled cover mocked her.

After a while she unlaced her dress and climbed in between the chilly sheets. It was such a large bed for one person. She curled up her knees, burrowing her head into the pillow, and fell asleep to the sound of her own quiet breathing.

She woke before dawn and for a moment gladness invaded her heart because Paget and Henrietta were not lovers and her jealousy had been unfounded. Then she remembered that Paget was in the Tower and that before the day was over she might very well be there herself. The shock of his arrest had numbed her senses as a rabbit is numbed by the glare of a stoat, but the shock was diminishing and her natural energy flooded back. She rang the handbell vigorously and at length Lettice answered, a wrapper over her nightgown, her feet thrust into carpet slippers.

"Is something wrong, mistress? It's scarce five o'clock!" she demanded, her voice slightly irritable.

"Wake up Mistress Henrietta and Robin and bring us something to eat," Abigail ordered.

"Now?" Lettice looked sleepily astonished.

"Right now. Without asking questions." Abigail made her voice brisk. "We expect to be away for several days, so tell Robin to saddle three horses – no, tell him to make it four lest one falls lame. Oh, do stop gaping and hurry!"

"Yes, mistress." Lettice fairly scurried from the room.

Abigail swung her legs over the side of the bed, forcing herself to think clearly. Lettice would have to be left in charge of the household. She would wear her topazes and the emerald ring so that, if necessary, she could bribe her way to an audience with the King. She splashed cold water on her face, combed back her hair and struggled into her russet gown and warm cloak.

"I've brought you some breakfast, mistress," Lettice said, coming in again. "Robin's seeing to the horses and Mistress Henrietta is already dressed. Is something wrong?"

"Master Paget is in trouble," Abigail said briefly.

"Henrietta and I are going to see what can be done. I shall leave you in charge of the house. Henrietta will give you the keys."

"Is Master Bailey to be told?" Lettice asked.

She had forgotten about the steward. John Bailey would have to be told something, she supposed, but she shrank from telling him the whole story.

And there was Thomas. If she told the King the whole truth then he would certainly be arrested. A little wistfully, Abigail remembered how she had sewn her wedding gown, how pleased she had been with the simple turquoise ring. She had been young and silly then, but those had been happy days and she couldn't bear to spoil their memory by too ruthless a betrayal.

"I'll call in to see John Bailey myself," she decided.

"It will be all right, won't it?" Lettice asked. "There seem to be so many things happening."

"Everything will be fine," Abigail said reassuringly.

The oatcakes and ale and cream cheese tasted strange at this early hour, but she found, to her own surprise, that she was hungry. At least she had embarked on some positive action, and that alone made her feel better.

The meal finished, she pulled up her hood and went swiftly down the stairs. Henrietta and an extremely inquisitive Robin were already mounted in the stable yard, and she mounted up herself, lifting her hand to Lettice who hovered anxiously in the doorway.

"I have to call at Master Bailey's house," Abigail said. "I have a message to deliver to him."

Henrietta looked a question but said nothing.

As they rode into the darkness Abigail couldn't resist turning for a last look at the house. It had been her home for a very short time, but she would never forget it, for within those walls she had grown from a foolish girl to a woman.

As they rode across the fields towards the steward's house the darkness began to lift, spreading silver across the grass. The harvest had been gathered and the corn was stacked in golden bouquets along the stubbed ruts. The apples on the trees hung in thick clusters ready for the plucking, and in the high meadow the cattle grazed, their sides sleek and padded after a good summer.

There was a light burning in a lower window of Master Bailey's house, and as she hurried up the path the door opened and the steward himself came out.

"Mistress Abigail, I was just now going to set out for Delaney Court. Master Griffin's servant rode over late last night saying that Master Paget was seen on the London road with two strange gentlemen. He said nothing to me about taking a journey, and I confess I am disturbed."

"May I come in for a few moments?" she interrupted, motioning Henrietta and Robin to stay where they were.

"Of course, of course, mistress. Do come in! Shall I get you some wine? It's a chilly morning," he said.

"Nothing. I ate before I left." She went with him into the small parlour where a fire had been kindled.

"Something is wrong, mistress?" He was gazing at her in concern.

"I want you to do a favour for me," she said.

"Of course." He indicated a chair but she shook her head.

"There isn't time. Master Bailey, you said you were very fond of my mother when she was a girl?"

"My devotion has never faltered," he said.

"Then for her sake will you do me this favour and never speak of it again to anybody?" she begged.

"Yes, of course."

"Not even to Master Paget?"

"Mistress, you have my word," John Bailey said, looking more and more anxious.

"I want you to ride at once to Windsor. There's a hostelry there called the Crown and Anchor."

"I know it, mistress."

"There is a – a gentleman staying there by the name of Armitage. Giles Armitage. I have a message for him. Tell him that Mistress Abigail has gone to tell the truth to the King and he had best look to his own affairs. Can you remember that?"

"Yes, but—"

"No questions. Just deliver the message and then come back here. And we'll never speak of it again."

"I promise you," he said.

She gave a last look round the little room. There had been friendship here, and she had been grateful for that. Then she went quickly into the cool and silvery dawn.

CHAPTER THIRTEEN

"WE will take the London road," Abigail said curtly as she remounted.

"To Whitehall?" Henrietta's face bore a look of respect.

Abigail nodded, slapping Cora lightly with her crop. They ought to make a good time on such a fine morning, she reasoned. Paget had mentioned once that the King often rose early to play tennis or the new game of pall mall, and that at noon, when Council matters were finished, he walked or rode in public to give as many as possible the chance of seeing him. Perhaps her opportunity would come then.

"Mistress, what will you say to the King?" Henrietta was asking in a low voice.

"I shall know how to frame my words when I see him," Abigail said. She wondered if he would remember her. It was very likely, after the exhibition she had made of herself at Court, that he would, and she doubted if he would be in any mood to listen sympathetically.

They rode steadily as the light strengthened and at any other time Abigail would have enjoyed the beauty of the sun-dappled leaves, the fresh breeze that blew away the last traces of morning mist, the spiders' webs that spun lacy covers over the hedgerows. This morning she could think only of frowning walls and damp dungeons where the air was foul.

"There are riders coming this way," Robin said abruptly.

They reined in their own mounts and listened. Within a few moments the thudding of hooves was clearly audible and a cavalcade of horsemen, muffled in cloaks, rode into their clearing and pulled up at the sight of the others.

Abigail recognised the King at once. There was no mistaking that heavy-lidded gaze, the ugly mouth, the luxuriant black curls, though he was clad in a heavy travelling cloak and broad-brimmed, feathered hat.

"Mistress Delaney!" His tone was one of drawling amusement. "Have you taken up highway robbery now, that you lurk about in the woods at this ungodly hour?"

"I was coming to Court," Abigail said, her face crimsoning with shyness. "I have a petition, sire."

"And I am bound for Delaney Court en route to a day's hunting at Windsor."

"You hunt early in the day, sir!"

"And have already netted a pretty wench, I see! Dismount and walk apart with me. I know your petition already."

She climbed down wordlessly as the King sprang from the saddle and motioned her away from the others. He was so tall that she had to tilt back her head to look at him, and it was with evident difficulty that he shortened his stride to match hers.

"Sire, my husband is arrested for high treason!" she said breathlessly. "And he is innocent."

"He's a fool, to take a Puritan wife and then to keep silent on her account!" the King retorted.

"To keep silent? Has he been put to the question already then?" The colour drained from her face.

"He spent a very uncomfortable afternoon in a draughty cell," the King informed her. "I interviewed him last evening, then left him to kick his heels under guard."

"Then he's not – hurt?"

"My dear young woman, we are not living in the days of my Tudor ancestors!" the King said impatiently. "Torture is officially abolished and I would countenance its unofficial use only in the most extreme circumstances. But word of a plot to kill me has to be investigated, you know."

"That list was found among my things. Paget knew nothing of it."

"Are you telling me that you are the one who should be under guard?" he demanded, pausing in his stride to look down at her. "You made your opinion of my court very plain when you came to Whitehall. You are of Puritan stock."

"I'm only a bit of a Puritan!" she protested. "My opinions are changing, truly they are! But I cannot think it wrong to be modest and to worship in my own way! Only I see now that dainty gowns and parties are not as wicked as I was bred to believe!"

"A bit of a Puritan!" he echoed. "Are you a bit of a traitor too?"

"No, sire!" Abigail shook her head vigorously. "That list and the plan for killing you were given to me by – by a man to whom I was betrothed. They were in a sealed package and he told me not to open them until Yuletide. I thought them tokens of affection – keepsakes!"

"And so hid them from your husband?" His lips curled cynically.

"I put them away, and forgot about them," she

rushed on. "The names on the list are false, sir."

"How do you know?" He shot the question at her so abruptly that she flinched.

"My – betrothed told me so. He made it all up because he wished to rid me of my husband."

"With your consent?"

"No, sire. If that were so I'd not have set out to ride to Whitehall."

"Hum!" He pulled thoughtfully at his underlip. "So you are guiltless too?"

"I ought not to have hidden the package, sir."

"That's true." He gave her another long look, and said, "I never believed the tale anyway."

"But Paget was arrested."

"I have to investigate when such allegations are made," he said. "However it did seem a little far-fetched that Paget Delaney should suddenly turn traitor after he had spent eleven years in exile with me, believing his father had disinherited him."

"You said you were coming to Delaney Court, sire," she reminded him.

"To inform you that your husband is considered by us to be a true and loyal subject. As we met you here then we are saved the necessity of turning aside and can continue with our hunting."

"Are you – are you going to arrest anybody else?" she faltered.

"For writing a farrago of nonsense? Or for hiding keepsakes from a husband?" He raised his eyebrows and gave his cynical, down-slanting smile. "I have more important matters to attend. My compliments to you, mistress."

"Your majesty." She hastily dipped into a curtsy as he turned and strode back to the others. Mounting, he gave her another faintly bitter smile, saying, "I left word that Master Delaney was to be released this morning, so you will have him home with you soon. Come! we're wasting good hunting time."

The royal party galloped on into the green depths of the woods.

"We can go back," Abigail said. "The necessity for going to Whitchall is over."

"Is Paget cleared of the plot?" Henrietta said.

"There never was a plot," Abigail said wearily. "We'll ride back."

She ought to have felt relief and gratitude for all their sakes, but she felt only an immense tiredness. It was good to know that Paget would be coming home, but she also knew that she could not return to Delaney Court. She was the last person Paget would want to see.

"I am going to visit Master Bailey," she said abruptly. "Robin, take Mistress Henrietta back to the house."

She would have liked to say goodbye to the young woman who had turned out so differently from Abigail's first impression of her, but she could not risk arousing suspicion.

"Are you sure you're all right?" the other asked.

"Perfectly. Go and catch up on your sleep."

She spoke lightly, swerving away from them across the meadows. By now John Bailey would have left for Windsor. She would wait for an hour then ride on herself. Where she would go was a thought that nagged at her mind. She dare not go to her parents, and she had no desire to follow Thomas Wellborn.

Vaguely she thought of making her way to the nearest port and taking ship for the New World. Her topaz necklace would surely pay for her passage, and she had the emerald ring to sell. Paget would certainly have the marriage annulled when he knew she had deserted him.

Master Bailey had left, but his bustling little housekeeper admitted her, accepted without question her request for hot water and showed her to the low-ceilinged bedchamber under the eaves which was obviously the steward's own room.

"Were you wanting something to eat, Mistress Delaney?" she enquired. "I've fresh bread and some tasty quince preserve."

"Nothing. I'll just freshen myself and then ride on," Abigail told her.

The water was fragrant and pleasantly warm. She splashed it on to her face and hands and groped for the big soft towel. The sun was rising higher, its glow warming the apartment. It was going to be a beautiful day, and for a few moments she gazed through the window, down into the charming garden. Someone was riding across the fields, riding furiously. Abigail had a glimpse of a sweat-lathered horse and a dark face raised to hers, and then there was the pounding of fists on the main door.

She looked round frantically for some way of escape, but there was the sound of voices below and then footsteps running upstairs. The door was wrenched open and Paget strode in, banging it behind him. He was clad in his rumpled travelling clothes and his expression was ominous.

Abigail backed away nervously, the damp towel still in her hands.

"So now you're in my steward's bedchamber," Paget observed.

"Washing my face," she said meekly.

"Is there a drought over at the big house?" he enquired pleasantly.

"I wanted to think," she said.

"About what?" He gave her a quick, searching glance and said. "You are wearing the topazes. Why? No, don't bother to lie, I can read your face like a book. Topazes can be sold, can't they, and then you wouldn't need to throw yourself on your parents' tender mercies. Isn't that true? You didn't intend to come back to Delaney Court at all."

"How could I?" she flared. "How could I go on living there after what has happened? Henrietta told me about it – about the way she agreed to help you win your wager."

"I just saw Henrietta myself," he broke in. "She tells me that you believed the package was a gift from Wellborn, and that you were on your way to confess to the King when you met his majesty. He might have thought you guilty of treason yourself. Did you consider that?"

"I am past thinking about anything," she said, flinging down the towel. "I am confused and muddled, and I want to be let alone. Just to be let alone! And you ought not to be here yet. You're supposed to be under guard."

"I was released and set off for home at once," he said. "Home – that sounds a mite ironic, doesn't it? A man expects to find his wife at home."

"I was never your true wife," Abigail said. "This marriage could be annulled."

"So that you could run off and marry Thomas Wellborn, flourishing the topazes as a souvenir?"

"I don't want Thomas Wellborn!" she cried angrily. "He has even fewer principles than you have!"

"I could have told you that in the beginning."

"You could have told me many things!" she said bitterly. "Do you think I enjoy knowing I was married for a wager, that every time you were pleasant to me it was with the object of winning that wager?"

"I like to win," he said.

"When you intended to give the money to Henrietta as a dowry all the time?"

"Henrietta is proud and would not take charity."

"And what of my pride?" she demanded. "You tried to use me so that you could *win*!"

"I tried to make you love me," he interrupted.

"To win the wager!"

"Because I fell in love with you." He spoke with as much intensity as if he detested her. "Oh, I made the wager, but when I came to the house and met you, then I desired you."

"Lusted!"

"That too. It's an honest emotion, at least. But I respected you, and if Thomas Wellborn had stood up to my threats I'd have withdrawn my offer *and* gone on paying your father's wretched pension! But Wellborn was not the man for you. I knew I could make you happy, but you found out about the wager."

"And you didn't explain."

"Because you wouldn't have believed me. You were determined to hate me from the beginning, weren't you?"

"You made it very easy!" she flashed.

"So you rushed off to the man who hoped to walk across my scaffold to the altar with you?"

"I never dreamed he intended such a thing, else I'd never have kept the package. You must believe that."

"It makes no matter," he shrugged. "I've lost wife and wager."

"You won't force me to return to Delaney Court?" She was so surprised that she gaped at him stupidly.

"I've never forced an unwilling woman," Paget said. "I'll escort you to Windsor and then see a lawyer. These matters take time, but we'll conduct the affair with as much dignity as can be managed. I'll not have my wife riding alone all over the countryside."

"That's very generous of you," she said meekly.

"Generosity costs nothing," he said tightly. "If you're rested now, we can start."

Abruptly, humiliatingly, her eyes swam with tears. Paget was giving her exactly what she wanted, without argument, and she was completely and utterly miserable.

"The topazes," she said, bending her head to fiddle with the clasp.

"They are yours. I take nothing that I gave," he said.

And he had given her so much. The bedroom that he had made so welcoming. She could see now that it had been intended as the perfect setting for the consummation of their love. And now it was all gone. She was walking away from it and he was allowing her to go.

"If you're quite ready?" His voice was icily polite but the vein at his temple throbbed.

"There is one thing," she said, and her voice was no more than a thread of sound. "The wager – you didn't lose it. I did fall in love with you, you see, and I hated Henrietta because I thought she was your mistress. Oh, I know it's too late, but I wanted you to know, so you can give Henrietta her dowry. That's all."

"*All*?" He walked slowly towards her, his hand reaching to trace the curve of her cheek. "And if I believe you, cannot you believe me when I tell you the wager meant nothing after I had met you? Cannot you even try to believe?"

He was so close she could feel his breath on her face, and the brilliance of his eyes pierced her soul, stripping away the last vestige of distrust.

"Would you like to make a new wager?" she asked softly, and slid her arms about his neck.

"Later," said Paget, and his kiss blotted out the world.

AVAILABLE THIS MONTH

DEAR LOVER ENGLAND

by Pamela Bennetts

Blessed with beauty, brains and wealth, Damaris Wyngarde seems destined to win Queen Elizabeth's favour when she joins the court as her youngest maid of honour. Yet nothing is as she expected – she finds the Virgin Queen torn between the demands of love and majesty, and her whole court racked by intrigue.

Even the gentle love of Hugh Saville becomes less important to Damaris than her own feelings for the forbidding Lord Randal Cavendish, although he seems to have nothing but contempt for her. And as terror threatens her sanity and even her life in this bewildering court maze, Damaris suspects that he may be trying to kill her . . .

December's other memorable Historical novel of romance, intrigue and excitement – order your copy today!

Old-fashioned value at 60p net

Masquerade
HISTORICAL ROMANCES